Too Sexy for Marriage
Cathie Linz

Harlequin Books

TORONTO • NEW YORK • LONDON
AMSTERDAM • PARIS • SYDNEY • HAMBURG
STOCKHOLM • ATHENS • TOKYO • MILAN
MADRID • WARSAW • BUDAPEST • AUCKLAND

If you purchased this book without a cover you should be aware
that this book is stolen property. It was reported as "unsold and
destroyed" to the publisher, and neither the author nor the
publisher has received any payment for this "stripped book."

ISBN 0-373-44039-1

TOO SEXY FOR MARRIAGE

Copyright © 1998 by Cathie L. Baumgardner

All rights reserved. Except for use in any review, the reproduction or
utilization of this work in whole or in part in any form by any electronic,
mechanical or other means, now known or hereafter invented, including
xerography, photocopying and recording, or in any information storage
or retrieval system, is forbidden without the written permission of the
publisher, Harlequin Enterprises Limited, 225 Duncan Mill Road,
Don Mills, Ontario, Canada M3B 3K9.

All characters in this book have no existence outside the imagination of
the author and have no relation whatsoever to anyone bearing the same
name or names. They are not even distantly inspired by any individual
known or unknown to the author, and all incidents are pure invention.

This edition published by arrangement with Harlequin Books S.A.

® and TM are trademarks of the publisher. Trademarks indicated with
® are registered in the United States Patent and Trademark Office, the
Canadian Trade Marks Office and in other countries.

Printed in U.S.A.

Once upon a time there lived the Marriage Makers—three fairy godmothers. Their job was to look after all the triplets in their domain, including the Knight triplets. One by one each fairy sprinkled her dust...

The first fairy godmother sneezed and covered baby Jason *(Too Sexy for Marriage)* with more purple and silver fairy dust than he ought to have had, giving him too much common sense and sex appeal.

The second fairy godmother, convinced she could do better, ripped open the lid of her container, spewing gold and emerald green dust all over baby Ryan *(Too Stubborn to Marry)*, bestowing him with an overdose of humor and stubbornness.

The third fairy godmother imperiously produced a velvet pillow, edged in fringe, that she tipped, sprinkling baby Anastasia *(Too Smart for Marriage)* with midnight blue and fiery red. Anastasia would be the one with intelligence and a little too much attitude.

Could they all live happily ever after?

Dear Reader,

We have so many goodies for you this month, I barely know where to begin! Longtime reader favorite Cathie Linz has joined the Love & Laughter lineup with a very special trilogy called MARRIAGE MAKERS. Susan Elizabeth Phillips says, "Cathie Linz's fun and lively romances are guaranteed to win readers' hearts! A shining star of the romance genre." Jennifer Greene adds, "Every book has sparkle and wit; Cathie is truly a unique voice in the genre." Cathie is also the winner of the *Romantic Times* Storyteller of the Year Award as well as having been nominated for Career Achievement in Love and Laughter. Her trilogy about the Knight triplets includes lots of emotion, comedy and the antics of some well-intentioned but bumbling fairy godmothers. Don't miss *Too Stubborn to Marry* in June and *Too Smart for Marriage* in September.

Bullets over Boise is a fabulous comic mystery from bright new star Kristin Gabriel. Caterer Carly Weston wants to be famous for her meat loaf, not for dead bodies in her kitchen. Still, being the star witness in a murder trial means she needs the expert protection of Agent Jack Brannigan. Only, Carly prefers seeing sexy Jack wearing an apron rather than a gun....

Don't miss these two very special and wonderful stories.

Malle Vallik

Malle Vallik
Associate Senior Editor

Dear Reader,

Who doesn't love a good fairy tale? I know I do. When I was a little girl, the first movie I ever saw was *Sleeping Beauty,* and I can still remember thinking the princess had great hair and the prince was really cute. But I was most impressed by the fairy godmothers and the colorful magic they possessed. This quickly became my favorite fairy tale and my favorite Disney classic.

My fondness for fairy godmothers continues to this day, which is why I'm so delighted to be working on this very special trilogy with Betty, Muriel and Hattie Goodie— a trio of novice fairy godmothers who each have an attitude and know how to use it. They are not as proficient, however, with their magic…as you will soon see. Everything that can go wrong does. But these intrepid fairy godmothers are nothing if not persevering in their quest as marriage makers who must unite true soul mates.

So sit back, kick off your shoes, keep some chocolate-chip cookies handy and be prepared to meet a man who is too sexy for marriage and the woman who gets caught up in a bet that she can snag him. I hope you enjoy reading Jason and Heather's story as much as I did writing it!

Happy reading,

Cathie Linz

For Meg Ruley,
Agent of the Century
who believes in
magic.
Thanks for
believing in mine
and
sharing the dream.

Prologue

"HOW HARD CAN THE JOB be?" Betty Goodie demanded of her two sisters.

"The responsibility is tremendous," Muriel Goodie stated solemnly.

"Does this hat go with this dress?" Hattie Goodie fussed with the bluebird on the wide brim before daintily patting her silver curls in place. "Maybe I should have worn my lilac gown instead. Is this shade of blue the right color for a christening?"

"Look," Betty said sternly, "let's just focus on the matter at hand, shall we?"

Hattie, the resident worrier in the group, leaned over the church balcony railing to ask, "Are you sure no one can see us up here?"

"Of course they can't see us," Betty snapped, shoving the bangs of her Prince Valiant haircut off her forehead. "We're fairy godmothers, for petunia's sake. It's our job to be invisible."

"And it's our job to look after all the triplets born in our domain," Muriel added. "Oh, dear, look...the poor Knight triplets are crying."

"What a racket!" Betty exclaimed, clapping her hands over her ears and nearly jabbing herself in the eye with her magic wand. "Let's do our job and get out of here."

"Don't be so cavalier about this," Muriel scolded. "We have to do this right, or else!"

"Or else we're out on our fairy godmother bottoms." Betty glared at Muriel. "I know that. Try and make me nervous, why don't you?"

"We're nervous because this is our very first day on the job," Hattie noted, as she smoothed her frilly sky blue gown. "Not that our predecessors didn't have the right, after 250 years, to retire...oh, dear, this flying is such a tricky business," she added as she bumped into the head of a gilded angel hanging high on the church wall. She grabbed the carving before it tumbled in the sunbeams streaking through the stained glass windows and fell onto the small crowd gathered below. Batting her wings as she rehung the ornamental object, she peered down over her shoulder to say, "I do hope the gentlemen can't look up my skirt with me hovering up here like this."

"I told you, they can't see us." To prove her point, Betty swooped down and buzzed around the minister's head three times before shooting back up to bestow a gloating smile upon Muriel.

"Show-off!" Muriel's sniff was disapproving.

"Fussbudget!" Betty retorted. "Stop imitating a stiff-necked stork and let's get this show on the road." Being the oldest of the Goodie triplets, Betty was used to giving orders and even more used to having them obeyed.

Tugging on her left ear lobe with one hand, she concentrated on materializing the all-so-important fairy dust into the palm of her other hand. With a showy flash, a glass jar appeared right on target.

Betty's triumphant look continued as she easily opened the container.

"You store your fairy dust in a grape-jelly jar?" Muriel asked with a disbelieving shake of her head.

"Never mind that." Hattie's voice quivered with excitement. "This is our moment to shine!"

Instead, it was Betty's moment to…sneeze.

Sparkling fairy dust, in shimmery silver and regal purple, settled over one of the babies wrapped in a blue receiving blanket.

"Now look what you've done!" Hattie wailed. "You got dust on my dress!"

"Forget your dress, what about the baby?" Muriel said in an apprehensive voice. "That dust is *powerful*. It affects the entire future of the babies, regulating their personal characteristics. We were told over and over again how important it was to dispense it in just the right proportions!"

Betty shrugged. "So baby Jason Knight gets a little more silver and purple than usual…what characteristics do silver and purple control, anyway?"

"Common sense and sex appeal," Muriel replied.

"Works for me," Betty said.

Muriel was infuriated. "How are we ever going to get this job done when you can't even do a simple thing like shake out a little fairy dust? You're not taking this seriously enough, that's the problem," she muttered in disgust, the spiky tufts of her short white hair sticking up from her cowlick and giving her the appearance of a woodpecker. Reaching inside one of the myriad pockets of her photographer's vest—her favorite attire—she lifted out a compartmentalized container that looked like it should have been in a chemistry lab. "Unlike you, I store the tools of my trade properly. All I have to do is open the lid and..." She paused to struggle with the stubborn hinge.

"You were saying?" Betty smirked.

"All I have to do is open the blasted thing..." Muriel angrily braced the container against her ample bosom and put all her strength into yanking the lid open. "Aha!" she exclaimed triumphantly, once the obstinate lid finally gave with a suddenness that caused a hefty amount of the contents at the far end of the container—glittering gold and intense emerald green dust—to fly out.

"Nice going," Betty said mockingly. "A direct hit on baby number two, Ryan of the powerful lungs— listen to that little guy scream—who just got over-dosed with what?"

"Too much from the humor and stubbornness end of the characteristic scales, I fear," Hattie noted with a shake of her head. "Really, girls, I can't believe how the two of you have botched this job. Let me show you how it *should* be done."

"Fine, Miss Smarty-pants," Muriel retorted. "Let's see you do it."

"Well, to begin with, presentation is everything," Hattie stated with an airy wave of her magic wand. As always, her wand matched the color of her dress.

With the second wave of her wand, a royal purple velvet pillow edged in a golden fringe appeared in midair. The top of the pillow was draped with elegant folds of sheer chiffon shot with strands of gold and purple threads. Nestled in the midst of all this splendor was a glorious gilded vessel adorned with cherubs.

"Now that's more like it," Hattie noted, taking her eyes off her creation long enough to shoot her two sisters an imperious look.

The small break in her concentration was just enough to disturb the floating pillow's precarious balance, upsetting the elaborate vessel with its fairy dust along with it.

Alarmed, Hattie reached out to make a grab for it. But all she ended up accomplishing was a somersault in midair that would have made a gymnast proud. The hem of her frothy sky blue skirt caught on her hat as it drunkenly tipped over one of her eyes, leaving her to helplessly watch the overabundance of midnight blue and fiery red dust pour daintily down upon the youngest Knight triplet, Anastasia.

"Oh, horsefeathers!" Hattie exclaimed when she finally managed to right her hat, her dress, and herself. Peering down at the wailing baby girl, she said, "You know, those two colors do make a lovely shade of plum. I wonder how too much intelligence and attitude will work on a girl?"

Disconcerted, the fairy godmothers gazed down at the havoc they'd unwittingly caused.

As the poor parents looked on in dismay, baby Anastasia cried and waved her hands, smacking the poor minister on the nose as he bent over her. Propped against his father's shoulder, in between gusty wails, baby Ryan would pause to grin at some inner joke. Baby Jason, held in his frazzled mother's arms, looked very disapproving of the entire thing as he joined his siblings in their painfully loud vocal outburst.

"I can tell you one thing," Betty noted, tugging

on her snowy bangs with a heavy sigh. ''I think we're going to have our hands full with these three! If we don't go deaf first!''

1

Thirty-three years later, 1998

"YOU LUCKY DOG, you! Normally when I eat here it takes me ten minutes just to get a waitress's attention. Today I'm with you and we've got four waitresses hovering around us at all times."

"Maybe if you tipped better, you'd get better service," Jason Knight retorted, giving fellow attorney Gordon Metcheff a reprimanding look meant to shut him up. It didn't work.

Gordon might look like a blond choirboy, but he had the heart of a shark.

"This has nothing to do with tips," Gordon said, raising his eyebrow as he sat back in the booth. The restaurant was located near the courthouse and hadn't been redecorated since Kennedy was president. The red flocked wallpaper was showing signs of wear, but the food in the place was not only good but quickly served, important for lawyers with harried schedules. "This has to do with you being named Chicago's Sexiest Bachelor."

"Why don't you say it a little louder? I think there are still a few in the back who might not have heard you the first time."

"Can I get you some more coffee?" a perky brunette server asked, leaning close to Jason to show him her cleavage. He could have sworn she'd undone another button on her white blouse since the last time she'd stopped by their table, four minutes ago. She'd also written her name and phone number on a paper napkin and slipped it to him with his grilled chicken sandwich.

"No, thanks. We're fine," he said, giving the waitress a no-nonsense look that he hoped would kill her ardor, for once and for all. Couldn't a man enjoy his lunch in peace?

"I'm glad to hear that. I like my customers to be fine. And you certainly do qualify as being fine." She gave Jason a blatant once-over. "If you need anything, you just give me a whistle."

Jason just shook his head in dismay as the waitress sashayed off, moving her hips in a way that made Mae West seem demure in comparison.

"Who can whistle?" Gordon groaned. "My mouth's dry."

"That's because your tongue is hanging out." Jason impatiently tapped his fingers on the tabletop. "Can we stick to business here?" Gordon worked in the public defender's office, and Jason's work as a prosecutor in the district attorney's office meant they were on opposing sides in court. "I thought we were having lunch to discuss the Fiarelli case."

"Later. First let me bask in this spotlight you've got shining on you," Gordon said, ogling the women who were ogling their booth.

"Some spotlight," Jason grumbled as two women in another booth giggled and pointed at him.

Gordon was not sympathetic. "Hey, if it happened

to me, I'd be shouting the news from the rooftops. What a brilliant way to meet babes. So how does it feel?''

"I admit that at first it was…interesting, but now it's interfering with my work. My desk is covered with strange mail reeking of perfume. Would you believe that I actually got some woman's underwear in the mail yesterday? She sent them to me along with a photo of her modeling them.''

"Were they thongs, by any chance?'' Gordon was practically drooling onto his roast beef sandwich. "Please tell me they were thongs.''

"Can I get you some more ice water?'' another waitress, a blonde this time, inquired in a husky voice.

"No.'' Jason was curt with her, seeing as she'd already spilled several ice cubes in his lap because she'd been batting her eyelashes at him instead of paying attention to what she was doing. Luckily, the water pitcher had been practically empty at the time. "No more ice or water.''

Pouting, the waitress flounced away.

"Let's get back to that photo,'' Gordon suggested. "Clearly it upset you. The least I can do is take it off your hands for you. Do you have it with you? You better give me the underwear, too.''

Jason was not amused. "This is no laughing matter. Do you have any idea how much ribbing I've taken at the office? I mean, I like a woman's attention as much as the next guy, but there's such a thing as too much of a good thing.''

"I wouldn't know. Women aren't exactly lining up to go out with me,'' Gordon said, grimacing.

"They were lining up at the health club to use the

exercise bike next to mine. It was embarrassing. I could kill my sister for doing this to me.''

''What's your sister got to do with it?''

''She's the one who sent in my picture to *Chicagoan Magazine*.''

''And they published it without your authorization?''

''No. It turns out the publisher is a college buddy of our illustrious district attorney.''

''And since you're a rising star in the D.A.'s office, you didn't want to rock the boat by refusing to let your boss's friend run your picture and crown you Chicago's Sexiest Bachelor.''

''That's it in a nutshell.''

''Then take my advice, buddy.''

''Which is?''

''Sit back and enjoy the attention while it lasts. And be sure to pass any women you don't want in *my* direction.''

''PSST, WAKE UP!'' Heather Grayson whispered to her friend and radio producer, Nita Weisskopf, as the two of them sat in the far corner of the crowded conference/break room. Several of the smaller tables had been pushed together to form one long table around which most of the staff of WMAX sat in various stages of attentiveness. Latecomers like Heather and Nita were relegated to the back, near the refrigerator that was on the blink. ''The meeting is almost over.''

''I'm wide-awake,'' Nita whispered back.

Heather wasn't buying that for a minute. ''You were snoring.''

In her late forties, or so she said, Nita was a

bleached blonde with golden skin and strong eyebrows. Both tough and glamorous, she had innate style, confidence and moxy. She might have been able to con most of the people in that room, but not Heather. That alone had made the two of them bond immediately.

"So the bottom line is that throwing money out the window really *can* pay off," station manager Tom Wiley droned, "as our most recent promotion, Throw Me the Money, proved. I confess I had my doubts about our morning crew tossing ten-dollar bills out the window to settle a bet about the Cubs' losing streak last year. But for a mere five hundred bucks, we snared coverage for WMAX Radio on all of Chicago's major television stations and in half a dozen papers. We made our fans happy, even if we did tick off the cops doing crowd control. Good job. And now I'd like to end this staff meeting by giving more kudos."

Heather tried to appear attentive, but Tom's monotonous voice was enough to put a hyperactive kid to sleep.

Besides, she already knew what was coming. The kudos always went to self-proclaimed "Doctor of Sportology" sportscaster Bud Riley. Each week it was the same. Management gushed, Bud grandstanded and then the meeting finally ended.

"There's one person here today I'd like to single out, someone who has been especially valuable to this radio station. Someone who we think is going to continue to improve some already great ratings, someone who has a natural talent and a devoted following...."

Bud actually preened, not an easy thing for a mostly bald man to do.

"So please join me in giving an enthusiastic round of applause to…"

Bud was already on his feet.

"Heather Grayson," Tom continued. "Host of our hottest afternoon show, *Love on the Rocks,* where relationships are stirred, not shaken."

Bud sank to his chair in disbelief, while Heather almost fell out of hers for the same reason. This had never happened before. Bud always got his generous serving of flattery at the end of the staff meeting. It was a given, a no-brainer.

"Stand up, Heather," Tom instructed, even as Nita jabbed a friendly elbow in her side.

Heather stood, self-consciously tugging on her baggy sweater. She'd forgotten today was Tuesday, staff meeting day, and had chosen an outfit that was put together with comfort rather than fashion in mind. Which is why she'd been sitting in the corner.

"Say something," Nita prompted in a whisper.

"I don't know what to say."

"Right." Bud snickered. "Not knowing what to say, that's a great trait for a radio personality to have."

"I save the good stuff for my show," Heather said, glaring at Bud's head. God, his scalp was so shiny, you could use it as a mirror. She shuddered at the thought of ever getting that close to Bud's head or any other part of him.

"Well, keep up the great work, Heather," Tom said. "That's it, gang. Until next time…"

If looks could kill, the one Bud gave Heather would

have had her requiring immediate CPR. He was clearly not a happy camper. Since his latest divorce he'd become even more impossible than usual.

Heather had tried to be understanding. After all, it couldn't have been easy for Bud to have his young "trophy" wife leave him to run off with her personal trainer. But Bud had a way of repelling all offers of sympathy or friendship. In the nearly four years she'd worked at WMAX, he'd rebuffed all her gestures of friendship until she'd stop offering them. Heather disliked labels, but "office bully" fit Bud to a *T*.

His latest victim had been Cindy, the new secretary. "You call these letters?" He'd ripped them up in front of her nose. "I'm not sending out garbage like that to my fans! Next time type them exactly the way I tell you to."

As a tearful Cindy had dashed out of the room, Heather had taken up the secretary's cause. "Couldn't you have cut her a little slack? She's only worked here a week."

"Mind your own business!" Bud had snapped before stomping off to his office.

Bud hated the fact that Heather wasn't intimidated by him. But growing up as the ugly duckling in a household of goodlooking people had given Heather a unique perspective on life in general and insecurities in particular. No doors had been opened for her; she'd had to struggle with each one of them by herself. Even so, she'd managed to successfully cross every threshold with a zest that had become her own trademark.

Heather had worked her buns off to get where she was today—the host of her own talk show. She'd put her heart and soul into the program. She'd come up with the show's title and conceived the format, a phone-in talk show that offered advice with a twist of laughter to the romantically challenged.

Humor was something that got Heather through life. And it would get her through this latest confrontation with Bud, who liked to brag that he'd attended the Howard Stern School of Sensitivity.

"You want to know what I think?" Bud sneered, his trademark gravelly growl interrupting Heather's thoughts. "I think you're pretty pathetic."

Heather smiled at him, a surefire way to throw him. "What a coincidence. I was just thinking the same thing about you."

"What would a woman like you know about relationships between men and women?" Bud continued. "It's a joke. It's not like you've got any credentials."

The man was an attack dog. "What would you call my master's degree in psychology and communication?" she said, feeling herself lose control and not caring one bit. Damn Bud and his sarcasm!

"A boondoggle. You're not a shrink or anything. And you certainly can't be drawing on your own experiences in life because we all know you don't have a life to speak of."

This was a sore point with her. Okay, so she *hadn't* had a date in a month of Sundays. But she'd had relationships in the past. They'd just never worked out.

Traditionally Heather had a soft spot for artistic types who needed a lot of attention. High maintenance, Nita had called them. There had been Patrick, the Irish poet, and Neil, the intense playwright. They'd appreciated her support, her encouragement, her bed, but in the end, the man in her life still eventually walked off into the sunset with someone else. Maybe it was her fault. She made bad choices, fell for guys with no desire to settle down. It didn't help that the someone else they ran off with was usually prettier, skinnier and sexier than her—someone like her own head-turning, gorgeous sister Erica.

Her sister lived in Arizona now and Heather didn't see her that often. Last year, their parents had moved out to join Erica.

Heather's entire family voiced their pride in her success in radio broadcasting while in the next breath saying they wished she'd "try to do more with her looks" as if it was somehow her fault that she wasn't the beauty they wanted her to be.

"I do have a life, Bud, and I do know what I'm talking about." Heather hated the fact that she sounded more than a little defensive.

"Then prove it," Bud demanded in front of the staff remaining in the conference room. "If you're such an expert on love, relationships and men, then you should be able to figure out a way to snag any guy you want."

Bud's scornful tone made it clear that he presumed Heather wasn't going to grab a man with her looks. In fact, she was the first to admit that without makeup she was bordering on average. She knew every physical fault in detail—her thighs were too big, her face too square, her brown hair too bland.

But her personality was memorable, as was her voice, and she'd made the most of both in her career in radio broadcasting. How many times had she heard the comment, "You don't look at all the way you sound"? Too many times.

"What's the matter, Bud?" Heather countered. "Nothing going on in the sports arena today? No one hitting any pucks?"

"We're not talking about me, we're talking about you, sweetie. You can talk the talk, but can you walk the walk, if you get my drift."

As if watching a tennis match, the staff's eyes all swiveled from Bud to her before zipping back to him again as he grabbed a copy of *Chicagoan Magazine* from the conference table. Holding it up, he pointed to the cover story on "The Sexiest Bachelor in Chicago."

"I dare you to snag this guy." Bud jabbed his finger toward the photo as he read the quote beneath it. "A tough nut to crack, this sexy prosecutor has his days filled bringing criminals to justice. It will take a clever woman to distract this serious legal eagle from his torts." Bud smirked at her. "You're a clever woman, right? At least that's what you're always telling me. So, I dare you to snag Jason Knight. I bet you can't do it."

Heather's gaze took in the expectant look of her co-workers. They were clearly looking for a show. Fine, she'd give them one.

Taking her time, she finished the remainder of her caffeine-laced soda before expertly tossing the can into the blue recycling container. "*Snag,* such a male word! What exactly do you mean? You expect me to marry him? Come on, Bud, if you're going to throw out a challenge, you've got to be more specific."

"Fine. I'll make it specific. You've got to get him

to go out with you. To a popular nightspot, like Andre's, where everyone can see you.''

"That's it? Dinner? You mean I don't even have to kiss the guy?'' Heather mocked, not taking any of this seriously.

"*He* has to kiss *you*. And not at the restaurant. Someplace less romantic.''

"How about a Cubs' game?'' one of the technicians suggested.

"How about the Ferris wheel at Navy Pier?'' another piped up.

"The Ferris wheel...yeah, I like that. That will do,'' Bud said. "And to prove that you have him eating out of your hand, you'll have to make him do something he's never done before. Something totally out of character for a serious...what did they call him?''

"A serious legal eagle,'' Heather answered. "How about in-line skating?''

"Fine. Think you can handle that? An intimate dinner date at Andre's, in-line skating and then making out on the Ferris wheel.''

"All in one night? Sounds like I'm going to be a busy woman.''

"In the interest of fair play, I won't insist it all take place in one night.''

"Oh gee, that's a relief. And how will you know I've accomplished these things?''

"Because Nita and I will be watching you.''

"I'm not into voyeurism,'' Nita protested, stepping closer to Bud, looking as if she was going to bop him.

"That's not what I heard,'' Bud retorted, stepping even closer, as if daring her to.

Sensing an impending fight, Heather stepped between the two. "And if we really wanted to make things interesting, we'd up the ante by saying that if I win, Bud would agree to be nice to the entire staff for the next twelve months."

"No problemo," Bud retorted. "There are two chances of you winning—slim and none. And slim just left town. The bet is on."

For the first time, Heather looked disconcerted. "Hey, I was just kidding! You've never heard of sarcasm?"

But no one heard her as the conference room erupted into a blaze of pandemonium, with everyone hastily placing their bets.

Never one to be shy, Nita immediately began recording the wagers as crumpled and crisp dollar bills were waved in her face.

"Twenty on Bud!"

"Five on Heather."

"Show me the money!" Nita shouted above it all.

"Well, here's another fine mess you've gotten yourself into," Heather muttered under her breath.

"I TOLD YOU she'd accept that bet," Betty said, gloating from her perch atop the fridge in the corner of the room. She was wearing a T-shirt that said Fairy Godmothers Can Fly Because They Take Themselves Lightly.

"I don't believe how much junk food they've got in this room," Muriel noted in disapproval as she hovered above the countertop nearby. The spiky tufts of her short white hair were even more disheveled than usual because of the brisk beat of her wings, a sure sign she was perturbed. "The sodium level in here is enough to open a salt mine."

"She didn't actually say she accepted," Hattie nervously noted, tugging on the lace veil of the pert cherry-colored hat that was an exact match to her Chanel suit.

Betty shrugged. "The result is the same. I knew she wouldn't let Bud challenge her that way."

"What makes you think Jason is going to like Heather?" Hattie asked worriedly. "She's not very glamorous, like the other women he's dated. Are you sure she's his soul mate?"

"I'm positive," Betty replied. "We checked the records three times."

"We do everything three times," Muriel interjected. "It takes us that long to get it right."

"Speak for yourself, fussbudget. Jason will like Heather just fine," Betty maintained. "If she can track him down. You know he never listens to us."

"Too much common sense," Muriel said. "And we all know whose fault that is."

Betty ended the discussion by tossing a pretzel in the air and batting it toward Muriel with her magic wand. Her slugger stance would have done Babe Ruth proud.

Luckily, no one noticed the snack flying through the air before Muriel caught it in a catcher's mitt that she'd pulled out of her vest pocket. Once in her possession, the pretzel became as invisible as she was. "Strike one," Muriel declared. "Remember, three strikes and you're out."

"Three strikes and we're all out on our fairy godmother derrieres," Hattie reminded them. "So quit fooling around and let's get busy."

2

NOT AN HOUR after the bet between Bud and Heather had been placed, Heather started receiving helpful hints from her female co-workers. The first suggestions came in the form of several Post-it notes fluttering on the computer screen in her cubicle.

"Pheromones. Hottest thing in perfume."

"Stock up on killer heels and bustiers."

"Dress for Sex," another said, but attached to it was a fourth Post-it disputing that advice.

"Sex too soon shrinks his excitement!!"

Another tip came in person from Linda Chin, who devised special promotions like Throw Me the Money. "A word to the wise. Wonderbra." She threw back her shoulders. "Makes a *big* impression."

"Don't fall prey to all this focus on outward attractiveness," Bev Stewart, the general sales manager, told Heather later in the ladies' room. "It's demeaning. You're better off using your brains rather than your body. Don't you change a single thing about yourself."

Heather was heartened by Bev's pep talk, only to learn later that Bev had placed fifty bucks on Bud. It was enough to make a woman's self-esteem take a nosedive.

"Hey, girl, let's go kick some butt," Nita declared, grabbing Heather on her way out of the building after work. "I've got five hundred bucks riding on this bet."

"The whole thing was a *big* mistake," Heather said.

"Too late now. Besides, this is our chance to rub Bud's face in a little of that manure he's forever spouting. Have you heard what he calls your show? 'The wimpy girlie show where broads bash men.'"

"I've heard. Where are you dragging me?"

"To Omar's."

"What's that? Some kind of harem preschool?"

"Omar's real name is Al, and he's a true miracle worker."

"Forgive me for being sensitive here, but I'm a little tired of hearing all afternoon about the miracles that will be required for me to attract Jason Knight. I'll have you know that I'm not a *totally* helpless case here. Even you, Ms. Devoted-to-Basic-Black, have to admit that I have great taste in clothes. Not today, maybe, but when I put my mind to it. Sometimes. On a good day."

"Remember what that caller this morning said. 'Guys don't want women with great taste, they want women that taste great.' And I'll have you know that I happen to love black because it's a no-brainer. Everything in my closet goes with everything else."

"You don't have a cat. Trust me, nothing black in my closet stays that way long. Not with my cat's long hair."

"The bottom line is that we need to punch up your looks, turn you into a powerful dude magnet."

"You might as well wish that I'd win Big Lotto while you're at it. I'm sure the odds of that happening are higher than me becoming a dude magnet, powerful or otherwise."

"Where's your positive attitude?"

"Someone stole it," Heather said.

"Well, I'm going to help you find it." Nita power-walked Heather around a corner of Michigan Avenue, beyond Water Tower Place. "It's not far now...ah, here we are."

Taking Heather inside a narrow building, Nita whisked her up an elevator that had to have been built shortly after the Chicago Fire. On the fourth floor, the doors opened to an opulent reception area decorated with Oriental rugs over tangerine carpet. The receptionist had three pierced earrings in each ear and a small gold stud above her right nostril. Her lime green blouse shimmered in the fluorescent lights, revealing the black bra she wore beneath it.

"I've got a bad feeling about this," Heather muttered.

"Nonsense," Nita said before turning her attention to the receptionist. "Tell Omar that his greatest challenge has arrived."

"More like Mission Impossible," Heather commented.

"Nothing is impossible," a man in billowy, black silk pants and shirt dramatically declared as he entered the room with a flourish. "Come." He held open the door to the crowded inner sanctum of his salon. "Sit." He pointed to a chair in front of a mirror. Heather had barely sat down before he wrapped her, mummylike, in a protective cape. Staring into the mirror, he said, "You are a blank canvas. Nothing. But I will fix that. Like Picasso."

"I prefer those gentle portraits Mary Cassatt did to looking like one of Picasso's nightmares," Heather informed him.

"Nonsense. Gentle is out. Dramatic is in."

"So what do you think, Omar?" Nita asked, fluttering around like a nervous mother at a beauty pageant.

"I can't believe you're doing this," Heather protested to Nita. "You could have your NOW membership card burned for this, you know."

"This is about money, not feminism."

"I think cut the hair," Omar stated. "About here." Omar indicated a line above the top of Heather's ear.

Heather's strangled shriek of dismay was drowned out by the hairdresser's continuing diatribe. "And color it with some highlights. Contrasts. Perhaps orange henna. And we need to give it more height." He lifted her shoulder-length hair toward the ceiling. "We must make you look more like an urban-aggressive woman. I will go prepare."

"What do you think you're doing?" Nita demanded as Heather frantically tried to undo the restrictive cape wrapped around her.

"Getting out of here!"

"No, you're not. Do you know what strings I had to pull to get Omar to see you so quickly?"

"Forget strings, get me out of this straitjacket."

"Just calm down. Omar knows what he's doing. This is the trendiest salon in all of Chicago. Women would kill to be where you're sitting."

"I'd kill to get *out* of where I'm sitting."

At that moment a young woman walked by, exclaiming, "I look so much better now. You guys did a great job on my make-over." She spoke through lips painted with black lipstick and waved nails coated with matching polish. Her eyes were completely circled with brown shadow, giving them the hollowed-out appearance of a character in a horror flick. Her hair was short, cut in tousled peaks layered with alternating shots of orange and purple.

"I'm outta here," Heather declared, yanking the stubborn cape over her head and jumping out of the salon seat as if it were an electric chair. She opted to use the staircase to make her getaway, so Nita couldn't catch up with her.

"Talk about ungrateful!" her producer shouted down the stairwell.

JASON FELT AT HOME in a courtroom. Being there never failed to get to him. This was where he belonged, where he could make a difference.

In a court of law there were rules and regulations, procedures that needed to be observed. He loved the underlying sense of order, so different from the chaos of his upbringing. Here he felt in control.

While waiting to begin his closing statement to the jury, Jason happened to glance toward a woman in the public gallery's first row. She was staring at him fixedly and rapidly blinking at him.

At first he thought she was having trouble with her contact lenses, something he could sympathize with. It was one of the reasons he preferred wearing glasses. That and the fact they made him look more studious and less studly. At least that's what Sandra, the court stenographer, had told him.

Which was good. He liked studious. He'd rather be known as Chicago's most *successful* prosecutor than its sexiest. He needed to be taken seriously in order to attain the goals he'd set out for himself.

Jason had his life broken down into five-year plans, with specific target dates for all his goals. Married by age thirty-five, preferably to someone in his own profession, who understood the time demands his job placed on him and who shared similar goals. Three kids, a nice house in Winnetka. Running for a major political office by age forty.

So far, he was right on track careerwise, with a big promotion looming in the near future. Provided this Sexy Bachelor business didn't derail things. Sure, the district attorney thought it amusing, but Jason wanted to make sure that his boss also realized his value as someone who got the job done.

Once Jason began his closing statement, his attention was completely focused. Until he happened to pause right in front of the public gallery where the blinking woman sat.

She was now pointing to her closed eyelids—on which she'd written "WANT U" in neon letters large enough for him to read. As she tilted her head down, he saw that she'd actually shaved his name into her shortly cropped hair.

"Is there a problem, Counselor?" Judge Rhinelander inquired at the pause in Jason's eloquent presentation.

"No problem, sir." Just another day in court for Chicago's most aggravated bachelor.

HEATHER DIDN'T FEEL she was truly safe from Nita's version of the hair police until she was home with the door to her condo closed behind her and a bag of groceries in her arms. Only then could she relax.

Coming home always made Heather feel good. It had taken her years to save enough money to be able to afford a place like this. But the early scrimping had been worth it. Living here, on the north branch of the Chicago River, was a dream come true for her. She loved her home and had turned it into her own personal retreat from the world.

She'd done the decorating herself, and the overall feel was one of cluttered warmth. Most of the pieces in her living room, such as the red-and-white star quilt hanging on the wall, were one-of-a-kind, and each had a story of its own.

The back wall of the living room was almost entirely glass, showcasing a tranquil view of the river. From her brick terrace, Heather enjoyed watching the river traffic floating by. This time of year, early May, the terrace looked its best, filled with potted pink azaleas and dark red hibiscus.

Her shoes clattered against the pine floor as she kicked them off and eyed her off-white couch. Flopping onto it was tempting, but first she had food to put away.

Her cat, Maxie, was already in the kitchen, sitting in front of his dish, sending her a look that clearly said, "I know you've got tuna in that bag."

Heather had gotten Maxie two years ago when he'd been little more than a kitten, a homely runt no one had wanted. She'd looked into his hopeful eyes and had immediately known she'd be letting him into her home and her heart.

Leaning down to scoop him into her arms, Heather said, "You don't know the kind of day I've had. I barely escaped being turned into a walking example of an urban-aggressive female. I'm lucky I got home in one piece."

Maxie's response was a loud purr. Her ear was resting against the soft gray fur on his side, and she grinned at the motorboat rumble he was making. There was nothing like the sound of a cat purring to put things in perspective. It ranked right up there with hot fudge sundaes as something that instantly made her happy.

After feeding Maxie his special treat, she began unpacking her groceries and was surprised to find a package of hair coloring in the bag. How had that gotten in there?

Reading the box, she noted that the color was temporary and would be gone in six washings. A disastrous hair coloring nightmare in college had left Heather leery of repeating the experience, which was why she'd left her hair the way it was all these years, despite her mother's and sister's constant cries for her to "do something about your hair." In her book, bland hair was better than a fried scalp and dried-out locks. But after Omar's scathing dismissal of her as a "nothing," Heather felt a need to make a statement of her own in retaliation.

Two hours later she stared at her reflection in the mirror with amazement. Instead of her usual mousy brown, her hair was a luscious red. It fell in a smooth curtain to her shoulders, actually swishing as she turned her head to get a better look. She couldn't believe it had turned out so well. Her mouth was still too wide, but now it matched the dramatic flare of her hair. Even the strong lines of her square face didn't look as out of place as they had before.

She looked like a woman who could get any man she wanted. Well, maybe not. But at least she looked like a woman for whom it wouldn't be *totally* impossible.

Confidence surged through her, making her feel like Rocky winning his fight in the movie. "Yes!" she shouted, aiming a clenched fist toward the ceiling.

"THAT WAS CLOSE," Hattie clung to the bathroom light fixture to the left of Heather's bathroom mirror. "She almost knocked my hat off!"

"She missed you by a mile," Betty retorted from her perch on the other light fixture.

"Do you know what chemicals were in that stuff she put on her hair?" Muriel's expression was one of disapproval as she looked down on them from the top of the medicine cabinet over the toilet.

"Oh, horsefeathers!" Hattie said irritably, straightening the sunshine yellow picture hat that matched her dress. "I come up with the brilliant idea of putting that hair coloring in with Heather's groceries, even going so far as to pick the shade—"

"Russet is a kind of potato," Muriel interjected.

"—And do I get a word of thanks from either of you? No." Hattie sniffed like one who had been much put upon before smoothing out the wrinkle in her favorite white gloves, the ones that daintily buttoned at her wrist. "Not one single appreciative comment."

"That might be because you were acting like a flibbertigibbet in that store, nearly knocking over that condom display doing somersaults like that," Muriel retorted disapprovingly, the cowlick in her short hair sticking up even more than usual, as she put her hands on her ample hips and glared at her sister.

"Can I help it that I get excited when shopping? Besides," Hattie added with a shrug and a pat to her silver curls, "they should put things like that in a more discreet place."

"Quiet, you two," Betty ordered sternly. "The stage is set. Now all we have to do is sit back and wait."

"Wait for Jason to be united with his soul mate, his one true love." Hattie sighed and clasped her gloved hands to her bosom. "And then our mission will have been accomplished."

"At least with Jason. There's still Ryan and Anastasia," Muriel reminded her.

Betty said, "It's not enough that we have to watch over all the triplets born in region two in midwestern North America—"

"Which includes Naperville, Illinois, the triplet capital of the United States," Muriel interrupted.

"But we also have the further job of uniting them with their soul mates as adults." Betty's grumbling was accompanied by an emphatic wave of her magic wand. Luckily, it wasn't activated, or the cat sitting on the bathroom floor beneath them would have been turned into a frog.

Muriel ended up having the last word. "Hey, uniting soul mates is a tough job, but somebody has to do it."

"YOU HAVE REACHED the voice mail for Jason Knight. I'll be in court all day today, but I will be checking my messages. So leave one after the beep."

If Heather hadn't been at work, she might well have tossed the phone on the floor and stomped on it. As it was she made do with forcefully hanging it up. She was tired of hearing this same old message the past three days. She'd already left a dozen messages for Jason, none of which had been returned, including the one in her best Ed MacMahon voice saying, "You might have won a million dollars! Call 555-6300, extension 16!" He hadn't called. It was useless to try again. Time for Plan B.

Too bad she didn't have one. Yet. She impatiently tapped a finger on the photo of the man she'd been trying to track down.

Every hour that went by without her even being able to establish contact with Jason Knight made the odds against her in the office pool go up. Or so Nita had been eager to tell her. "I don't want to put you under any pressure or anything, but the odds are now ten to one. Your new hairdo improved your odds a bit, but now things are going against us. All the women in this office—except for Bev, and she doesn't count—are depending on you. We've got our money on you.''

And so here Heather was, at her desk staring at the *Chicagoan Magazine* with the photographs of Jason. They were actually the same photograph, but the one inside was a much larger version, allowing her to get a better look at her intended victim. She grimaced. The term *victim* made it sound like she was going to mug him or something, when all she wanted was a little of his time.

Still, Jason didn't look like a man who gave anything away easily. He was wearing a suit, white shirt and conservative tie. The reflection of his wire-rimmed glasses didn't allow her to see the color of his eyes. He had a Mount Rushmore jaw and the stiff posture of an uptight perfectionist.

What would Jason the perfectionist think about Heather's current surroundings? Her cubicle space was as cluttered as her condo, filled with personal mementoes. Postcards from friends filled every available wallspace. Gag gifts from listeners, like the miniature sports car and the well-endowed bronze horse sculpture, were perched on various corners of her desk, often used as paperweights on the various piles she had scattered from one end of her desk to the other.

By contrast, her cubicle-mate, Linda, kept her side simple and streamlined. Her desk was clean, with a Zen garden the only adornment. On the wall was one framed oriental print. With her shiny, long black hair that always looked perfect no matter what, Linda was as simply chic as her workspace.

Nita's cubicle was around the corner and resembled Heather's more than Linda's, although Nita had calendars of hunks instead of scenic postcards on her walls.

As if conjured up by her thoughts, Heather saw Nita coming toward her with a determined look that was a call to action. "Come on, you." Nita grabbed hold of Heather's arm. "It's quitting time and you need a night out to get some inspiration on how to attack this bet thing."

Heather dug in her heels as Nita tried to tug her out of her cubicle. "I'm not going back to see Omar."

"Don't worry. He's banned you from his salon. No, you need a night out on the town and I've got just the place in mind. A bunch of us are going. Not Bev, though, traitor that she is." Upon reaching the elevators, they met up with Linda, Cindy, and Bonnie the receptionist. "Anyway, I thought we'd all catch a cab and head on over to that new club that just opened on Rush Street."

"You only want me along so I can whistle for the cab," Heather noted as they reached street level.

Nita grinned. "I'm still trying to figure out how you do that."

"Trade secret." Once they were outside, Heather gave her trademark wolf whistle. Sure enough, traffic screeched to a halt as a taxi veered across three lanes of traffic to pull up beside her.

"Maybe you should try that whistle on Jason,"

Nita suggested as they all piled in the cab. "You could leave it on his voice mail."

Ten minutes later, Nita was hanging over the back of the front seat, supposedly giving directions, but actually flirting with the handsome Arab taxi driver, who was eyeing the new breast job she was flaunting. Then the taxi stalled with an abruptness that almost tossed Nita headfirst into the cabby's lap.

"No go further," the cabby announced fatalistically.

"I wouldn't say that, honeypie," Nita cooed. "You and I could go a little further if we wanted."

"That's it, Nita, be subtle. Play hard to get," Heather quipped dryly.

Cindy gulped as if she wasn't sure if it was safe to laugh aloud or not, but Linda and Bonnie had both been around Nita and her flagrant ways long enough to crack up.

The next observation came from the ever-practical Linda. "Listen, in case you didn't notice, we've stopped in front of Muddy's, which claims to have the best jazz in town. I say we go inside and check it out. All in favor, say aye."

A chorus of ayes coincided with a group exodus from the cab.

The nightclub was crowded. They were shown to a table in the far corner from the stage, where the five of them had to sit so close together that their knees bumped.

They hadn't been sitting there fifteen minutes when one of the hefty guys from the next table leaned over to Heather and initiated a conversation. "We're in town for the porcelain-fixtures convention. How about you girls? We'll buy you more drinks." His words were slurred, his smile lopsided.

"No, thanks," Nita said on everyone's behalf.

"Come on now, don't be standoffish."

"But we are standoffish. I'm Nita Standoffish and this is Heather Standoffish."

"So you two are related, right? You girls come here often?"

Heather felt like banging her head on the table, but there wasn't room. Their drink glasses and a bowl of nachos took up every inch of available space. The club was smoky and warm and the tipsy bozo at the next table was leering, making Heather wish she'd stayed home, curled up on her couch with a cup of Darjeeling tea and a good book. Then she looked toward the small stage, where the musicians were warming up, and saw him.

He was dressed all in black, jeans and T-shirt both. His dark hair fell over his forehead as he leaned forward to remove his instrument from its case. It was a...

"Sax," she said.

"Sure thing. Your place or mine?" the tipsy conventioneer replied, scooting his chair even closer to hers.

Heather leaned away from him. "What are you talking about?"

"You just offered me sex," the man claimed.

"I did not! I was referring to the sax player on stage."

"You were offering to have sex with him?"

"Yes, that's right." She hoped her outrageous comment would get this jerk out of her face.

It did, but his next move wasn't much of an improvement.

"Hey, bud!" The guy stood up to shout at the sax player on stage. "This lady—" he pointed down at Heather "—has got the hots for you. Tonight's your lucky night! She wants to have sex with you."

Heather wanted to slide under the table, but she was wedged in too tightly to move. The sax player lifted his head and looked right at her.

And that's when it hit her. She'd seen that face before—that Mount Rushmore jaw, now covered by a sexy, five-o'clock shadow. It was Jason Knight!

3

QUICKLY FLAGGING DOWN a passing waiter, Heather pointed toward the sax player dressed in black. "That man. I want that man—"

"You and half the women in here," the waiter exclaimed.

"I meant I want to know his name."

The waiter, who sported a crewcut and trendy goatee, just shrugged. "He's not part of the band, he just jams with them sometimes."

"You don't know his name?"

"All I know is that they call him the Dark Knight and he drinks a specialty German beer."

Dark Knight? As in Jason Knight? It *was* him.

Well, Heather had wanted to get Jason's attention, and for a moment there she'd gotten it. She certainly hadn't planned on having some conventioneer yell across a crowded nightclub that she wanted to have sex with Jason. But the bottom line was it had worked. The Dark Knight, aka Jason Knight, had indeed looked her way, and she'd felt the electricity clear down to her toes.

Heather was amazed at what a difference glasses and a suit and tie made in the man's appearance. In that magazine photo his dark hair had been brushed back from a face devoid of emotion. Now his hair fell over his forehead as he closed his eyes and put the sax to his lips, coaxing the sweetest sounds from it.

Heather was entranced. The crowd around her faded into a fuzzy background and her attention became fixed upon Jason—the movement of his body, the fluidity of his fingers, the movement of his lips against the instrument. His dark T-shirt fit him to perfection, allowing her to watch the rise and fall of his breathing as he played his heart out.

The sweetly sorrowful music spoke to her soul. There were other musicians playing, but she didn't notice them. She saw only Jason, standing in a pool of light. She heard only Jason and the soaring notes he was creating. She felt the melancholy mixed with the message of hope he was conveying without saying a word.

So engrossed was Heather that she wasn't aware of the passage of time until the house lights went up again as the musicians finished their session. Dazed, she joined in the heartfelt applause around her.

Then she leaned toward Nita and said, "That's him."

"Him who?" Nita asked.

"Him, Jason Knight."

"Get out of here. He doesn't look anything like the uptight, legal eagle photograph in that magazine. What's in that Pink Squirrel you're drinking?" Nita held up the glass and sniffed the contents suspiciously.

"I'm telling you it's him. I know it. I can feel it in my bones."

"What you're feeling isn't in your bones," Nita retorted. "Didn't they teach you anatomy in that fancy university you attended? It's called lust. That guy is dangerously good-looking. And you know what that means. He's probably either gay or married."

"Okay, I admit that the demographic pool of good-looking, straight, single men is an increasingly small one, but I'm telling you that man up there is Jason Knight."

"If that really is Jason Knight, the editors of *Chicagoan Magazine* should have shown a picture of him dressed like that, all in black. They would have sold ten times as many copies. I can't believe you recognized him. I sure wouldn't have. So, what's your next move?"

"To get his attention."

"Honey, the conventioneer at the next table already took care of that for you."

"Who knew an offer of sex shouted across a crowded bar would do the trick?" Heather murmured dryly.

"Hey, it works for me every time." Nita grinned.

"Do you think he'll come over here?"

"Not if those bleached blondes at that table down in front have anything to say about it."

Heather belatedly noticed the two girls waving their hands at Jason. "He seems to be ignoring them. Uh-oh. It looks like he's packing up to leave."

"Then go get him, girl. We, the women who make the wheels go round at WMAX, are counting on you."

"WHAT, YOU LEAVING already?" Natron Jones asked Jason. He was big, black and the most talented horn player Jason had ever heard. He was also a good friend.

"Yeah," Jason replied. "I've got a full day in court again tomorrow."

"What about the redhead in the back who wants to have sex with you?"

"She has red hair, huh?"

"Man, are you telling me you're not wearing your contacts again?"

"I play better when I can't see the audience. That way I can concentrate on the music."

"Well, how about concentrating on that redhead in the back? She's not your usual type."

"What is my usual type?"

"Cold and in control."

"There's nothing wrong with control," Jason maintained.

"If you were so into control, you wouldn't play with so much emotion. This woman coming at you looks like the emotional type. Here she is. Don't squint at her, man."

"Jason Knight, we meet at last."

Jason was stunned. No one in the audience knew his real name. To them, he was only known as the Dark Knight. And he liked it that way.

Despite Natron's advice, Jason squinted at the woman. Her sexy voice sounded familiar to him, even if her features were a blur. He had to get her out of there before anyone else overheard her using his real name. He certainly didn't want a horde of women invading Muddy's, his last private refuge. Playing the sax gave him the only peaceful moments he'd had since this ridiculous Sexiest Bachelor thing had begun.

"Let's get out of here," he growled.

"Do I detect a testosterone power surge?" she inquired with a smile. At least Jason assumed it was a smile. Without his glasses he couldn't be sure. Maybe she had gas pains from one of Muddy's red-hot appetizers.

"A testosterone power surge, huh?" Grabbing his instrument case, he aimed her toward the exit as quickly as possible. "You seem the kind of woman who'd have surge protection."

She curled her fingers around his bare arm to stop him in his tracks. He could tell her touch wasn't driven by outrage. He could also tell that he liked being touched by her.

"And you seem like the kind of man who'd want to avoid walking into a pole," she noted dryly, tugging him out of the way of the upright metal support beam near the doorway to the club. "Maybe you should put your glasses on now." There was a tinge of laughter in her voice. "Before you hurt yourself."

Outside, with his wire-rim glasses firmly in place, Jason finally got his first clear look at the woman who'd threatened to blow his cover. Her hair was longer than many women favored these days, but it was the color that caught his attention. Maybe it was the artificial light from the streetlamp that did it, but her hair was like liquid fire.

And her smile was brighter than the megawatt illumination on the corner. She wasn't beautiful, but her face had a certain something. She had the strong jaw of a woman who knew what she wanted in life. Her lips were luscious, full and sensual, giving her the kind of mouth that was meant for leisurely hours of French kissing.

"Who are you?" he asked suspiciously.

"I'm the voice on your voice mail, remember?"

He'd been getting a lot of calls at work from strange women since that stupid article with his picture had shown up in the press. He'd ignored them all.

But he did remember this woman's voice. It was hard to forget. Kind of husky like Lauren Bacall's.

"Your glasses aren't just for effect, are they?" she noted.

"I don't do anything for effect."

"That's noble of you." Putting on the wire-rimmed glasses should have made him appear more distant, more uptight. But putting glasses on a sexy panther didn't turn it into a pussycat, she discovered. The underlying dangerous seductiveness was still there, coming across loud and clear.

"Why was it you wanted to see me?" Jason asked. "You never said in your messages."

Heather was tempted to reach out and muss up his hair. As if the fates were reading her thoughts, a sudden breeze sent his hair tumbling back over his forehead. That was better. Now he looked like the Dark Knight again. In fact, he looked so good that Heather had second thoughts.

She didn't like people who were too good-looking,

and this guy certainly qualified. They made her feel even more plain than usual. And they tended to be self-absorbed and selfish. Her family members were prime examples. But she didn't have to like Jason Knight, she just had to go out with him three times. Was that so hard? All the women at the radio station were counting on her.

This was fieldwork. That's how she needed to look at it—as research. No big deal. She was a successful woman with a fantastic job and a riverfront dream condo. She could manage this assignment, no problem.

Yeah, right.

"Why did you want to see me?" Jason repeated impatiently.

Why was it she was always wearing a baggy sweater and floral skirt when something important happened to her? If she'd known, she'd have worn one of her power suits, something to make her feel confident. Too late now. "Listen, can we stop someplace nearby for a cup of coffee? My treat. No strings attached. Then I'll tell you what it is I want."

Boy, this asking a guy out, even if just for coffee, was harder than she thought. Her palms were sweating and her deodorant was working overtime. She vowed to go easier on her next male caller who was nervous about asking a girl out. "Look, there's an espresso bar across the street," she added. "What do you say?"

"What do I say?" Jason repeated. "That I'd be a fool to refuse an offer like that."

"I'll bet I've aroused your curiosity, huh?"

"That's one way of putting it," he noted, while holding open the door to Jumpin' Java for her.

"Order anything you want," she said as they stood in front of the polished wooden counter. The menu was listed on a chalkboard on the back wall. "I'll have a decaf double mocha *latte* with cinnamon and whipped cream on top," she decided.

"Give me whatever's got the highest caffeine content," Jason requested. "I've got work to do yet tonight."

"That would be Arabian mocha java."

As they collected their drinks, Jason said, "You know, I can still remember when our only choices were decaffeinated or not. Ordering coffee used to be a no-brainer."

"Like wearing black all the time. I didn't mean you," she said, belatedly realizing he might misconstrue her comment. "A friend of mine always wears black so that she doesn't have to think about what goes with what."

"I do the same thing. This table okay?" He nodded toward a corner, where they wouldn't be disturbed. Once they were seated, he said, "So what did you want to talk to me about?"

"Can we just make small talk for a while first?"

Jason put his right hand to his glasses and lowered his head to give her a Tom Cruise *Risky Business* look over the metal rim. Then he smiled. The man had dimples! A flash of one, anyway. "Small talk, huh? Sure. If that's what you want."

She wanted entirely too much at the moment, and it was messing up her thought processes. She had met handsome men before so why did she feel like a tongue-tied idiot?

She'd already almost burned her tongue when he'd given her that look and incredible smile a moment ago. Her taste buds would probably be numb for a week. So what would it be like to kiss him when her taste buds were numb? Would he bring them back to life, stimulating a miraculous recovery?

She had to say something, had to get her mouth moving with words before she did something stupid, like lean over and kiss him. "Uh, what that guy said back at the club, it was a misunderstanding. I was talking to him about your sex—your *sax*," she corrected, so quickly that she was sure he hadn't noticed her slipup. Until she got another "look."

"You read the article in *Chicagoan Magazine*," he said, sighing.

"After looking at the pictures, yes. I mean, yes, I did read it, but only after a friend made me. Wait, that didn't come out right."

"I wouldn't have read it by choice, either."

"It wasn't so bad. The worst they called you was a tough nut." Her gaze lowered to his jeans and how well he filled them out. Jeez, why didn't she just plaster a sign on her forehead that said Sex Fiend? Eyeing a man's private...*attributes* ten minutes after meeting him. She'd never done that before. But then tonight marked a number of firsts for her. Quickly looking away, she added, "They also said you were a legal eagle. Good at what you do." Probably damn good at kissing, too.

"I am."

Had he read her thoughts? "You are?"

"Good at what I do. At being an assistant district attorney."

"Right. I knew that. About your work, I mean. Of course that's what I mean. I wouldn't know about you being good at other things. Except sex...the sax. I really like the way you played." And looked.

She took another sip of coffee. Thank goodness she'd gotten a decaf; she was already bouncing off the walls as if on caffeine-induced overdrive. She had to calm down and remember her mission.

"Are you ready to tell me what this is all about or do you want to continue with the small talk?" he asked.

"Continue with the small talk, definitely. Talking is my specialty. When I was a kid, my parents didn't know how to keep me quiet. They're elegant and beautiful, but not the chatty type. I love them, but they were downright stumped by me," she said cheerfully. "I guess I've got too much...I don't know, joie de vivre. Maybe I got my parents' portions, too. You know, when they give out traits at birth. What do you have too much of?"

He gave her a startled look before eventually replying. "Common sense. Or so my sister with the attitude is forever telling me."

"So you have a sister. I have one too. Any other siblings?"

"I've also got a brother."

"And are they older or younger than you?"

"They're both the same age as me."

"Same age? You mean you're...?"

"One of a set of triplets, yeah."

"Wow. I've never met a triplet before. Do your siblings look just like you?"

"My sister doesn't, much to her relief," he noted with a grin that flashed like the sun on a cloud-filled day. "We all have brown hair and eyes, but we're not identical. I suppose you could tell that we're related, but that's about it."

"Do they live here in Chicago?"

"My sister does. My brother is out in Oregon at the moment."

"So tell me, what was it like growing up as a triplet?"

"Crowded."

She laughed, and the sound made Jason want to test his theory about her mouth being made for French kisses. Normally, he hated small talk, but he liked the sound of her voice. There was a throaty sexiness to it that got his attention and kept it. And her laughter was even better. Rich and raspy with a touch of sugar.

"So being a triplet was crowded. Anything else?" she prompted.

"No. Mostly crowded. That's about it."

"You're not a man of many words, huh?"

Jason just shrugged.

"Then how did you end up in the law? I thought lawyers talked all the time."

"We do. At work. I'm not a work now."

"I talk a lot. You may have noticed. I especially talk when I'm nervous. Which is a good thing, actually, because if I wasn't good at talking I'd be unemployed. It's part of my work."

"Hey, aren't you Heather Grayson from that *Love on the Rocks* show on the radio?" a busboy with a skinny mustache asked as he collected empty coffee cups from the table beside them. "I saw your picture in a flyer my girlfriend brought home the other day. She's a communications major. You're giving a speech at Loyola later this month, right? Something about women on the radio."

"Yes, that's right," Heather said, smiling.

"You look much better in person. Wait 'til I tell my girlfriend. Like, she'll freak."

He was gone as quickly as he'd appeared.

Jason didn't look pleased. *"Love on the Rocks?"* Even his voice had changed. So had his demeanor. The Tom Cruise naughty gleam in his eye was gone. Instead, Jason looked almost…Republican. As if he were back in that conservative suit and tie from the magazine layout. "Does this invitation to have coffee with you have something to do with your radio show?"

"Why would you think that? Have you ever listened to my show?"

"No."

"I have the two-to-six in the afternoon time slot. The show has a call-in format. I don't have guests, unless they're specialists in relationships. Are you a specialist?"

"At prosecuting cases, yes."

"Well, I don't need anything prosecuted. So you can relax." Wanting to change the subject and regain their earlier camaraderie, she said, "Tell me what made you choose to play the saxophone."

"It chose me."

"Really? I like an instrument that knows its own mind. My cat is like that. He chose me. I was minding my own business, watering the azaleas on my terrace. I live on the north branch of the river and I've got this big terrace with great eastern exposure.... Anyway, he just showed up on my terrace and demanded that I be his slave."

"Nice work if you can get it."

"The thing is you can't own a cat."

"It's not allowed in your building?"

"No, I mean there's no such thing as owning a cat. It's more like they own you. And the funny thing is that you're happy to have it that way. Now, if we were talking about a male-female human relationship with these kind of dynamics, I'd say it wasn't healthy. But it's not as if a cat is a freeloader. They contribute a lot to the relationship. They don't give their trust easily, but when they do, it's wholehearted. Like when my cat lies on his back, with his eyes closed in ecstasy like this...." She squinted in a good imitation. "He actually smiles with his eyes while nurdling his claws."

Jason wasn't sure what "nurdling" was, but he got the general idea from the way Heather curled and flexed her fingers to demonstrate what she meant. Her movements gave him plenty of other ideas, too, all of them as steamy as an espresso machine. The woman was turning him on by talking about her cat! No doubt about it, he had gone too long without sex.

Jason still had no idea why she'd invited him to have coffee, but the bottom line was he didn't care.

He wanted to spend more time with her. He'd never
met another woman quite like her. Maybe it was that
joie de vivre she'd been going on about before. Or
maybe it was her throaty golden voice or her sexy
hair or the electricity generated by her touch. Whatever it was, he wanted to experience more of it...and
more of her. *All* of her. Every luscious inch.

4

HEATHER WAS RELIEVED that Jason seemed in no hurry to get home to that work he'd said he had to do. She had to confess she was enjoying talking to him, even if he was too good-looking for comfort.

Just when Heather started to relax and enjoy herself, Jason made use of a pause in their conversation to suddenly ask, "So are you ready to tell me what you wanted to talk to me about yet?"

What would he do if she said no, she wasn't ready yet and never would be? Maybe she should just throw herself at his mercy and tell him the truth. Gripping her coffee cup with her nervous hands, she shot him a hopeful smile. "How do you feel about betting?"

He frowned. "I don't approve of it."

Scrap that plan. "Then how do you feel about dinner? At Andre's. To discuss..." She racked her brain for something they could discuss, but her mind suddenly went blank.

Jason took pity on her. He placed his hand over hers. Then he smiled. The man had dimples. A flash of one, anyway. "You don't do this very often, do you?"

"Accost strange men and ask them out? No. And trust me, I wouldn't be doing it now if not for…"

"Yes."

An idea suddenly came to her. More like an excuse, really. The additional research she'd done on Jason came back to her just in the nick of time. "If not for our mutual interest in Safe House and domestic abuse victims. I know you've supported the organization in the past and I'd like to do something on my show, maybe help them raise some funds along with awareness."

Now that she thought of it, it did sound like a good idea. Why hadn't she come up with it before, before she'd bumbled around like a tongue-tied idiot, practically telling him her life history? Maybe because she did her best speaking behind the safety of a microphone in the solitude of a broadcasting booth. Where no one could see her face or her body; where they could only hear her voice.

She was all set to continue her pitch when Jason said, "Okay."

"Okay?"

"You sound surprised that I agreed."

"I am," she said frankly, before hurriedly catching her verbal slip. "I mean, I am delighted that you agreed. When would be good for you?"

"Tomorrow night too soon?"

Any night would be too soon as far as she was concerned, but better to get this over with as quickly as possible. "That would be fine. I'll meet you there at eight."

THE PHONE BEGAN RINGING the moment Jason let himself into his north side loft. He was subletting the place from an old law-school buddy who'd been transferred out of town.

The advantage of living here was that the open floor plan with its minimalist furnishings allowed for plenty of elbow room, leading up to floor-to-ceiling windows showcasing an impressive view of the city's skyline. The disadvantage was that noises reverberated in the open space like an echo chamber and the phone was no exception. Grabbing it, he tossed his briefcase onto the black S-shaped couch.

"So have you forgiven me yet?"

"Who is this?" Jason said, wincing as his keys fell to the floor, creating another sharp burst of sound.

"Very funny. It's your sister."

"Oh, right." He kicked off his shoes before sitting on the leather couch, his gaze automatically focusing on the blinking lights atop the John Hancock Center out the window. He liked its constancy. Every night the same. Off on. Off on. "The one who sent in my photo without permission."

"Give me a break." She had the gall to actually laugh at him. "I'll bet you're secretly enjoying all the attention from being labeled one of Chicago's sexiest bachelors."

"Not until tonight," Jason let slip, and then cursed himself as his sister immediately picked up on his words. He could practically see her antennae vibrating, honing in on what he might be up to.

"Really? Am I interrupting something?"

"Yes," he said impatiently. "I've got work to do."

"Work?" She sounded very disappointed.

"That's right." Swinging his briefcase onto the coffee table, Jason opened it and started thumbing through the stack of file folders inside.

"I thought you said something about enjoying the attention."

"That's for tomorrow night," he said absently, balancing the phone on his shoulder while his main attention was on the stack of paperwork still to be completed that night.

"Aha! You met a woman."

It was not a question, Anastasia said it as if it were fact, which irritated the heck out of him. For as long as he could remember she'd taken great pleasure in irritating him, saying it was her way of repaying him for being so bossy, which was ridiculous. He was not bossy. As a kid, he'd just been trying to keep order in a household that valued chaos.

Reluctant to give her the satisfaction of being right, Jason calmly said, "I meet women all the time."

"Not women who catch your attention or whose attention you want," she replied, sounding positively smug. "So, what's her name?"

Jason sighed. While he was reluctant to give his sister even the tiniest bit of information, he knew from experience she'd just hound him until he did. "Her name is Heather."

"Hmm. Sounds like a fluffy name."

"Right," he scoffed. "Like Anastasia isn't a fluffy name?"

"Hey, it's a *regal* name. Mom's been telling me

so ever since we were kids. But let's get back to Heather.''

"Why this sudden interest in my love life?''

"It's not sudden,'' Anastasia denied.

"No, that's right. You've always been nosy,'' he grumbled.

"I like butting into your life as much as you like butting into mine.''

"Not that you ever listen to me anyway,'' Jason retorted, running his hand through his hair, feeling increasingly frazzled by the second.

"You've got that right.''

"So why are you calling me? Just to generally harass me? Or did you have something specific in mind?''

"Harassing you would be reason enough, but I'm also calling because Mom and Dad are bickering worse than usual since he retired a few months ago.'' Anastasia's voice turned serious. "Mom says he's driving her nuts being under her feet all the time, criticizing everything she does. I think you should give them a call and talk to Dad, before things blow out of proportion.''

"Our parents have been bickering for as long as I can remember and it's never hurt their marriage. But I'll give Dad a call sometime soon,'' Jason promised in a preoccupied voice, his attention already centered on the file folder opened in front of him. "In the meantime, I've got work to do and not enough hours to do it in.''

"My brother, fighting for truth, justice and the American way. Sounds like business as usual to me.''

"Then keep your nose out of my business." Jason was smiling as he hung up on his sister. It was childish, but he liked having the last word.

"WELCOME BACK to our final half hour of *Love on the Rocks*," Heather said into the microphone, almost running over the swirling hem of her brightly-colored floral dress with the wheels of the chair as she quickly shifted her position. She'd already ripped several dresses with that maneuver, not to mention once running over her big toe. Each time she vowed to be more careful, but then she'd get involved with what she was doing, dealing with the hundred-and-one intricacies of putting on a show. The dim lighting in the booth was intended to keep her attention focused on the console in front of her—command central with enough blinking lights, slides, buttons and knobs to give NASA a run for their money. "We're talking to Jane from Joliet. Before the break, you were telling me that you do and do and do for this new guy in your life and all you're getting in return is doo-doo. Sounds like a bad deal to me, Jane. Kind of like trading in a Lexus for a Pinto, you know what I mean?"

"But he's so cute."

"Looks aren't everything."

"That's what you think."

Heather leaned forward in her chair. "Let's get back to this guy. You said before that you had a great relationship with someone else who you dumped to go with this current man who makes you miserable, takes advantage of you, borrows money, sees other women. Do I have that right?"

"It doesn't sound good when you put it that way."

"That's my point." Heather's voice was persuasive. "The final decision is yours, Jane. All I can say is that you might want to give that great-relationship guy you dumped a call and see if he's moved on to someone else."

"He wouldn't!"

"Someone else might have snatched him up by now," Heather added, feeling a definite affinity for the man. She definitely knew how it felt to be used.

"He's not that cute."

Heather's affinity went up another notch or two as she said, "But he knows how to treat a woman right, and guys like that are worth their weight in gold. Am I right, ladies?" On cue, Heather added the sound of women chanting "Yes, yes, yes" by moving one of the slides on the console in front of her. She had several sound-effects cassettes all cued up and ready to go at a touch of her fingers. "There you have it, Jane. Good luck. And we'll be right back after these words."

During the commercial break, Heather sipped her coffee. Normally she was very focused on her work, checking in over the intercom with Nita, who was in the adjacent production booth, connected to the broadcast booth by a door and a big soundproof window.

But today, Heather was worrying about her dinner date with Jason. Miraculously, thanks to a last-minute cancellation, she had been able to get a reservation at Andre's. But she still hadn't decided what to wear.

She had a pink dress that looked good, but that was

before she'd become a redhead and she didn't think redheads were supposed to wear pink. She had a gorgeous lilac silk suit, but she never wore it while eating because she might spill something on it.

Oh, why had she gotten caught up in this mess? There was no way a woman like her could keep the attention of a man like Jason. She hadn't even been able to keep Howard's attention, and Nita had called him a "nerd extraordinaire."

After all the bad luck she'd had with artistic types, Heather's relationship with Howard had been a definite change of pace. He was a botanist, a rock solid scientific type. But even that relationship had blown up in her face six months ago when Howard came down with an early case of midlife crisis. Saying that he needed to find himself, he'd abruptly headed off to the South American rain forest with a curvaceous research assistant named Freedom.

Wherever Howard was, she hoped he was sweating and being eaten alive by mosquitoes. It was small of her, she knew, but she couldn't help herself. Howard's betrayal had hurt her the most of all because she hadn't seen it coming. She'd been completely blindsided. Artistic types weren't meant to be stable, but Howard had been the Rock of Gibraltar type. Or so she'd thought.

What was it with her and her taste in men? She always picked the wrong ones. While she might not have been crazy in love with Howard, she'd thought it was safe to care for him.

She *knew* it wouldn't be safe to fall in love with Jason. Not that she had a track record of playing it

safe as far as romance was concerned. But her heart
had been broken enough times. She didn't want to be
disappointed yet again.

It took her a moment to realize that Nita was waving a sheet of white paper in front of the glass with
the words "You're on!"

Heather put her hands to her headphones. Dead air!

Frantically leaning into the mike and almost knocking out her front teeth in the process, Heather hurriedly scanned the screen of the computer display in
front of her.

Nita was not only the show's producer, but also the
call screener, selecting which incoming calls would
go on the air and typing the necessary info onto their
computer link. *Line 3, Wendy from Winnetka. Strange
guy question. Wake up!!! Are you reading this??
Hello???*

Checking the console to verify her mike's volume,
Heather hurriedly said, "Sorry about that, folks. Our
next caller is Wendy from Winnetka. Hi, you're on
the air. What can we do for you today?"

"This guy I know does something kind of strange
and I wanted your opinion."

"Okay, but keep in mind that this is a show about
relationships, not sex education. For that you'll have
to check out Dr. Ruth."

Wendy giggled. "No, it's not that. It's just that,
like he…um, he loaned me this book of poetry. I
looked at it, but it was too heavy for me."

"Too heavy, huh? How much did it weigh?"

"About five pounds," Wendy replied with a smack
of her chewing gum. "Maybe six."

Dumb as a bunny! Nita typed on Heather's screen.

"Anyway, I gave the book back to him. Then he, like, calls me up and tells me he found a strand of my hair between two of the pages. He said he smelled it and it made him think of me. This guy is, like, just my college study partner. I don't see him that way, you know?"

"As someone you want smelling your hair strands, you mean? You're saying you don't feel an olfactory affinity with him."

"A what? An old factory?"

Dumber than a bunny! Nita typed.

"Olfactory means having to do with the sense of smell," Heather explained. "It sounds to me like this guy has a nose for romance."

"But he's sniffing hair. And it's not like it was on my head. It was, like, dead hair, you know? Don't you think that's kind of gross?"

"It doesn't matter what *I* think. It matters what *you* think, and from the sound of it, you think this relationship with this guy is going nowhere."

"Right."

"Then you should tell him that."

"But what if he stops wanting to be my study partner?"

"A risk you might have to take."

"But then I'd, like, totally flunk English."

"Perhaps, but you'd get an *A* in humanity." She gently noted. "Think about how you'd like it if someone used you just to get ahead. Trust me, I know how it feels." Neil, the playwright, had wanted to use Heather's contacts in the broadcasting business to get his work produced. "It hurts. So be gentle, okay? Thanks for calling, Wendy. And we're out of time. Thanks for tuning in today. Until tomorrow, this is Heather Grayson stirring things up with *Love on the Rocks*."

Miguel, the board operator in the production booth, added the show's traditional closing of ice cubes hitting a glass as a carbonated beverage was added.

"So tell me again how it went with Jason last night," Nita demanded as soon as Heather left the broadcasting booth.

"I've already told you ten times. It went well. I'm having dinner with him tonight at Andre's."

"Which means that Bud and I have to be there to witness the event." Nita paused in the hallway to stick her tongue out at Bud's PR picture hanging on the wall.

"Don't remind me." Heather rolled her eyes and groaned as she moved past Nita. "Like I'm not going to be nervous enough dealing with Jason."

"You were thinking about him when you messed up after the commercials, weren't you?" Nita asked, following Heather to her cubicle.

"Maybe."

"No maybes about it. I could see where meeting a sexy hunk like Jason would be distracting."

Heather gave Nita a reprimanding look. "I wasn't sitting there fantasizing about his body, if that's what you're insinuating."

"Of course not." Unrepentant, Nita perched on the corner of Heather's desk. "You were probably fantasizing about his hands. He has great hands, long and thin but not too small. Powerful.''

Heather tried taking the high road.''Actually, I hadn't noticed.''

"Liar. But hey, if you don't want to admit how sexy he is, that's your business. Just don't go missing any more cues during your show. You almost gave me a heart attack there.''

Heather hung her head and looked suitably remorseful. ''Sorry about that.''

"What you should be sorry about is your clothes.'' Nita eyed the loose-fitting floral dress Heather was wearing. ''I hope you're going to change before you meet him.''

"You're so good for my self-confidence,'' Heather noted ruefully.

"What you're wearing is fine…for work. Not for snagging. Snagging takes a different look.''

"Like the one that woman wore leaving Omar's salon the other day?'' Heather countered, rolling her chair away from Nita. ''Sexy and strung out, you could call it.'' She shook her head. ''Sorry, not my style.''

"How about something black and clingy?''

The suggestion made Heather laugh. ''Adorned with cat hairs? I don't own anything black and clingy. I do, however, own something purple and sort of clingy, and I plan on wearing that tonight. I'm actually starting to sort of look forward to it. Andre's is supposed to have really great food.''

"Forget the food,'' Nita advised. ''Concentrate on the man. And the bet.''

JASON WAS WAITING for Heather when she arrived at the restaurant. Andre's was fashionably current with plenty of swirling glass and elegant greenery. Swagged burgundy curtains stood out against stylish stretches of bare brick walls. Even the indoor fountain in the elegant foyer splashed with dainty class rather than sloppy gurgles.

Jason fit right in with the high-class surroundings. He was wearing a black suit, complete with gleaming white shirt and conservative burgundy tie. With his glasses on, it was hard to see any signs of the Dark Knight who'd so sweetly wooed her with the sounds of his sax at the club last night. But when Heather looked beneath the surface, there was no mistaking the rock-hard jaw or the slight downward slope of his brown eyes.

He wasn't waiting alone. Surprise, surprise.

A well-dressed blonde with big hair was hanging on his every word with more than casual interest. She was as perfect looking as he was, and it made something inside of Heather twist in painful awakening.

Not jealousy but insecurity. She'd walked into a room and felt this way before, too many times—when her sister, Erica, flirted with Bobby DelGreco in the eighth grade; when she stole Heather's boyfriend, Randy Smurtz, in high school; every year at their parents' Christmas party.

Actually, Heather had felt this same achy pang each time she'd looked at her perfect family and wondered how she fit in with all that beauty. The answer was that she didn't.

But that was then. This was now. And now she

was Heather Grayson, radio personality. No slinking back into the wallpaper for her. Not anymore.

Instead she glided forward—hard to do wearing killer heels, but she managed it—and gave Jason her best smile.

He smiled back.

And to her astonishment, the woman retreated in search of new prey.

"Was I interrupting something?" she asked.

"I've never met her before in my life. Thanks for showing up when you did and coming to my rescue." Before she could reply, he added, "You're not like other women."

His comment rankled. "Which means what?"

He shrugged. "Just that you're different."

She was different all right, Heather thought to herself as the maître d' lead them to their table. She wasn't just interested in Jason for his body. She was interested in him to win a bet. Which didn't exactly make her feel like a candidate for the Humanitarian of the Year award. In fact, she felt guilty as all get out. But she was determined to prove herself to Bud and anyone else who doubted her ability in the relationship department.

She was also determined to clear up a few things from the night before. "Look, about that scene at Muddy's, I don't want you thinking that I'm some kind of troublemaker, or that I get inebriated conventioneers yelling about sex every night," she said bluntly.

Giving her a quizzical look over the top of the

menu, Jason said, "You have something against sex every night?"

Her eyes widened, then she smiled. "Hey, you do have a sense of humor."

"Should I be insulted that you sound so surprised?"

"Not at all. I like surprises. How about you?"

"I'm not all that fond of them myself."

Great. He didn't like betting and he didn't like surprises. And he looked so handsome tonight that she overcompensated by not looking directly at him, something she hadn't done since grade school when she'd ignored Bobby because she didn't want him to know she had a crush on him. This was very mature.

"Do you know what you want to order or would you like some help?" Jason asked.

At this rate she'd need plenty of help, like having her head examined. Getting him to have dinner with her was one thing, getting him to kiss her was something else again. In her panic, she couldn't remember if he was supposed to kiss her here or while skating…or was it supposed to be on the Ferris wheel? She should have taken notes.

"Have you decided what you want?" he repeated.

Jason. Naked on a platter. The image exploded in her mind like a full-blown sexual fantasy. Where had that come from?

She immediately whipped out her mental remote control and switched stations to something more appropriate. She also did the soft *om* mantra she used whenever she got nervous before a show.

Remember, this entire situation is supposed to be

light and easy, no complications. Not that anything
in her life had gone easily or smoothly, so she supposed it was foolish to start thinking things would
change at this late juncture.

"You okay?" he asked her.

"You bet. Not that you do. Bet I mean. Let's start
all over. I'm Heather Grayson and you're?"

"Hungry."

Without further ado, they both ordered the orange
roughy with citrus hollandaise sauce, which turned
out to be a good choice. Their waiter served them
with smooth efficiency.

Jason turned his plate so that his carrots were at a
precise right angle to his fish, which was at six
o'clock on his plate while the potatoes were at nine
o'clock. Heather noticed the way he didn't let his veg-
etables touch his fish, keeping them meticulously sep-
arated. Very different from the way she dug into her
food.

Another example of how different she and Jason
were. He was great-looking, she wasn't. He had too
much common sense, she didn't. If she did, she'd
never have been suckered into this bet. She was no
good at this cloak-and-dagger stuff.

The oddly configured restaurant was large and very
crowded. More than one woman eyed Jason appreciatively as they sauntered by. To give him credit, he
didn't eye them back.

"This sexiest bachelor thing really does make you
uneasy," Heather noted in surprise.

"It seems pretty frivolous," he said, clearly em-
barrassed.

"But surely you must be used to women paying attention to you."

"Paying attention, but not mailing themselves to me. Some woman actually had herself crated and couriered to my office this afternoon."

She blinked in disbelief. "You're kidding."

"I wish." His expression was that of a man near the end of his rope.

"There, there." She patted his hand. "It could have been much worse. They could have done a calendar on you. Like the Studmuffins of Science calendar. Not that I own that myself, you understand. My producer has one on her cubicle wall."

He looked skeptical. "You're making this up, right?"

"No. She's got a couple calendars on her wall."

"I meant about the title of that calendar. Studmuffins of Science?" He raised an eyebrow.

"Featuring buns, biceps and Bunsen burners. I don't know if they have one for lawyers yet. If they did, they could feature buns, biceps and briefs. Or they could do torts and torsos and call it The Hunks of Habeas Corpus. No, Latin in the title probably would be rejected by the people in marketing. How about Sex Slaves of Sidebars? Boy Toys of Jurisprudence, Chests of Cute Counselors, Pecs of Prosecutors? Hey, you're looking a little green around the gills." She patted his hand again. "Don't worry Jason. By the time they have those calendars, you'll no longer be Chicago's Sexiest Bachelor. Some new young turk will lay claim to the title."

"That can't happen soon enough for me," Jason grumbled.

"I can understand why I wouldn't like being the center of attention, but you…"

"Wait a second." He held up his hand to cut her off. "Why don't you like being the center of attention?"

"Well, look at me. I'm hardly glamour material. Whereas you—"

"Whereas *I* like looking at you."

"Yeah, right. You don't have to say that," she assured him with a grin. "I wasn't fishing for compliments. Let's talk about you instead."

Jason shrugged, drawing her attention to his broad shoulders. "There's not much to talk about."

Ideally she'd rather draw Jason out by getting him to talk more about himself, but obviously he was a man of few words.

Now if he'd have been a caller on her show and she hadn't had to look at him, she could probably have come up with something brilliant. As it was, she didn't feel comfortable interrogating him any further, so she steered the conversation toward fund-raising ideas to help Safe House and its efforts on behalf of victims of domestic abuse.

Time flew by as she and Jason brainstormed various options. They worked well together, with complimentary skills rather than contrasting ones. Their creative juices were flowing so quickly, they barely noticed when the waiter whisked away their empty plates.

It wasn't until she paused to take a sip of her *latte*

some time later that Heather happened to glance up at the wall of mirrors decorating the back of the restaurant and saw Bud and Nita sitting at opposite sides of the crowded bar. Actually Nita had managed to snare a tiny table at the edge of the dining area, while Bud was hunched on a bar stool.

The sight of her co-workers brought her off the mental high she'd gotten from talking to Jason. He'd had some great ideas, and a practical way of looking at things, keeping suggestions within the realm of possibility. He was a man who could make dreams doable.

In trying to finish the last of her *latte*, Heather tipped her cup too far and ended up with whipped cream not only on her lips but on the tip of her nose, too.

She laughed self-consciously. "Jeez, you'd think I'd know how to drink from a cup by now."

Lifting his still-immaculate linen napkin, Jason leaned forward to carefully wipe her face for her. "You clean up pretty nice," he murmured, so close that she could feel his words as well as hear them.

"You're just saying that." Her heart actually *quivered*. Either she was having cardiac trouble or this guy really *was* Chicago's Sexiest Bachelor. She cleared her throat, afraid of sounding like a croaking frog. Workman's comp didn't cover female radio personalities being struck deaf and dumb by overexposure to sex appeal.

"Why am I getting the impression you don't believe what I'm saying?" Jason wondered aloud. "You don't think I'd lie, do you?"

"No. But your mom probably raised you to be polite."

"Something wrong with that?"

"No. I mean that you're not really lying, you were just being polite. Which is a great thing. Polite is good. Hard to find these days. I like polite. Are you going to eat that *biscotto?* Do you eat when you get nervous? Do guys do that, or is it a girl thing? Judging from the calls I get on the show, I'd say it's a girl thing. I'm talking too much. You should stop me, really you should. Before I say something else stupid."

Jason responded by leaning across the small table and kissing her. It was over almost as quickly as it had begun, but he caught her completely by surprise.

Speechless, she just stared at him, her thoughts consumed by the attraction zipping through her body like random tracers of electricity. She'd once read somewhere that kissing was two people tasting each other. Jason tasted strong and sexy, a blend of the coffee he was drinking with an underlying essence all his own.

But Heather couldn't pause to enjoy the moment because she was distracted by the frantic hand motions Nita was making. Thankfully her friend's performance was out of Jason's range of vision, but even so, it was only a matter of time before someone noticed her pantomiming motions, the same kind she used when producing the show. Except that Heather had never seen this particular gesture before, a rapid revolution with wiggling fingers.

Excusing herself, Heather murmured something

about visiting the ladies' room. As soon as she was out of Jason's sight, she wove her way around the various columns adorned with foliage until she finally reached Nita's table. Sitting in the chair across from her, she said, "You're supposed to observe, not direct and coach. You were practically holding up cue cards."

"I was just trying to help. Listen, Heather, you've got to admit that I have more practical hands-on experience with men than you do."

"You've got more experience than all the women in this place put together."

Nita preened. "Thank you."

"That doesn't mean you can stay here. You saw the kiss, you can leave now."

"As I was trying to indicate to you, you were supposed to have Jason kiss you on the Ferris wheel, not here at Andre's."

"So that's what that giant circling motion was for. Great. I was afraid of that." Heather was also afraid that she'd enjoyed Jason's brief kiss too much.

What kind of woman was she to lead Jason here under false pretenses? She knew the answer to that. She was a desperate woman.

If everything worked out, she'd win the bet and thereby defend her reputation as well as force Bud to be nice for a year. Plus, as a result of her talk with Jason, she had some great fund-raising ideas for Safe House. Thank heaven he hadn't simply told her to talk to them directly instead of involving him in the process.

Now all she had to do was keep her cool, her poise

and her sense of humor. And not spill any more food or drink on herself.

"Did you hear a word I said?" Nita demanded.

"No. Listen, I've got to get back to Jason."

"A real sacrifice, I know," Nita mocked. "Spending time with a gorgeous guy like that. And he's straight. Why couldn't Bud have made that bet with me?"

"Because he knew he'd lose. Stop drooling into your wineglass and go already. And take Bud with you."

As Heather got up and turned to leave, her attention remained focused on Nita. Heather never saw the waiter with the dessert cart. He wasn't expecting her, either. Their collision was inevitable.

5

JASON CHECKED HIS WATCH again, hoping that Heather wasn't ill. She'd been gone a long time and he was getting worried about her. Deciding he'd better check on her, he left their table to search for the ladies' room. But that wasn't as easy as it sounded. This restaurant had more ferns than a rain forest and they made navigating difficult.

"Hey, watch out!" Jason heard a waiter shout. Instinctively looking around for the cause of the disturbance, he saw a flash of purple silk between plant fronds. Heather?

It *was* Heather, her arms windmilling as she tried to keep her balance. She appeared to be hovering over a dessert cart that the waiter was frantically trying to put in reverse. Jason was there in an instant, hooking an arm around Heather and preventing her from taking a dive into the middle of a whipped-cream-covered key lime pie.

The waiter wasn't so lucky. Hastily backing up in an attempt to avoid the collision, he bumped into a couple who'd just returned from the seafood-and-salad bar. Their overloaded plates went sailing into the air. Hapless diners within a five-foot radius shrieked as chilled jumbo shrimps rained down on them, dropping into low-cut bodices, plopping into wineglasses and nestling in upswept hairdos. A woman seated nearby wisely dove under the table to avoid the chaos.

Several crab legs ended up adorning one man's shoulders like a seafood mantle of state, their giant red claws resting in perfect symmetry on either side of his startled face.

Meanwhile the abrupt reversal of the dessert cart resulted in several items sailing off the far edge. They fell at Heather's feet in quick succession.

Shuddering, she hid her face in Jason's shoulder as she clung to him. Holding her close, Jason patted her back soothingly before realizing her trembling was caused by the fact that she was desperately trying to hold back laughter.

"I'm sorry," she gulped. "Do I have any shrimp in my hair?"

"No. You miraculously avoided disaster."

"Other than stepping in it," she noted ruefully, looking down at her designer shoes. They were goners now for sure. She was ankle deep in calories—whipped cream, chocolate mousse, key lime pie and what looked like flan. Carefully shaking each foot, she managed to get rid of enough gunk so that she could walk without sliding...or squishing.

There was no sign of Bud or Nita, she noted with relief, while plucking a single shrimp from Jason's hair. The dark strands slid against her fingers, thick and enticingly touchable. Even in the middle of bedlam, he had the power to take her breath away.

"We'd better get out of here while the going is

good," Jason suggested, noting the disapproving look of the maître d', who was heading in their direction. Jason made quick work of paying their bill, leaving a generous tip, before hustling her out.

Once they were safely outside in the parking lot, Heather wiped away the tears of laughter that had been restrained too long. "I'm sorry. I'm not usually such a klutz, honest. I would much rather have eaten that pie than worn it," she added. "And I didn't mean for you to pay tonight. Dinner was on me."

"Actually, *dessert* was on you."

"You've got that right," she agreed, wiggling her pie-coated shoes at him. "I look like a clown. All I need to complete the image are big floppy galoshes and fuzzy orange hair."

"I wouldn't say that. You look kind of cute," he said, teasingly tapping the tip of her nose with his index finger.

Cute. A four-letter word in her vocabulary. *Cute* didn't snag men. *Sexy* snagged men. *Cute* only made them smile.

"I think it would be a good idea for me to give you a lift home instead of you catching a cab," Jason stated.

"Thanks. I think you might be right," she noted wryly. "Do you have any paper towels in your car so I can try to minimize the damage?"

He nodded and reached into the back seat before saying, "Here, sit down while I clean you up."

The low-slung, bucket front seat meant that Heather ended up with her knees almost at her chin as she tried to remove her strappy heels, perching her feet on the door ledge. His car, a sleek black model, still retained enough new-car smell for her to be extremely wary of messing it up. Hunched over, she fiddled with a particularly stubborn clasp.

"You're going to get a crick in your neck doing that," Jason said, brushing her hands aside. "Let me do it."

Hunkering down in the V formed by the open door and the body of the car, he made short work of removing her shoes. Then his fingers rested against her nylon-clad foot, the pad of his thumb gliding along the valley beneath her toes. "Are you ticklish?"

She shook her head. "What about you?"

"Not on my feet. Tickle me under my arms and I'm a goner."

Talk about goners, she was melting under his ministrations. The warm brush of his fingers evoked provocative thoughts of his hands sliding up her calves to her trembling thighs and beyond. And then there was the fact that her foot was resting upon his rock-hard thigh as he bent over her, like a modern day dark knight attending his lady.

"I think this would be easier if you took your stockings off," he decided.

Easier for what? she wondered. For him to seduce her? For her to seduce him?

The sensual tension went up a notch or two as she slid her fingers beneath her dress to her lacy garters, releasing the fastenings one by one. She slid her nylons down an inch or two before Jason took over, his fingertips skimming her inner thighs as he unrolled first one sheer stocking and then the other. He did so with leisurely dedication, as if revealing state secrets that warranted the most intense concentration.

She could feel the magic of it in the very center of her being. He didn't take any untoward liberties, made no crude advances. He simply touched her as no one had never done before, as if she were a price-less treasure.

Once her stockings were gone, Jason explored her now bare foot. She could feel his body's warmth ra-diating into her. She'd never known that the inner arch could be such an erogenous zone. He moved his fingers in a slow, sensuous circle across the sole of her foot. Her sensitized nerve endings vibrated with awareness from the tip of her toes to the back of her heel.

He was nothing if not thorough in his approach, drying each toe, his fingers sliding between each one, making her shiver with sensual hunger. When he set her foot back onto his thigh, her toes were within greeting distance of his zipper placket and his swell-ing masculinity.

If she moved her foot a little higher she could prac-tice that move she'd seen Meg Ryan use in the movie *Restoration*. If she shifted her foot just a little...and gained twelve tons of courage. A move like that was more in Nita's playbook than Heather's. She could practically hear her producer's voice saying, "Go for it, girl!"

By the time he'd finished the clean-up operations, Heather was breathless and ready to throw caution to the wind. Boldly moving her foot, she inched her way higher up his thigh, only to end up nearly kicking Jason in the crotch as he suddenly stood up.

Talk about a close call!

Jeez, wouldn't that be just her luck, to debilitate a man when she was trying to seduce him. Sneaking a look at his face, she was relieved to see that he had no idea how close he'd come, one way or the other, to heaven or hell.

Her quick glance lingered, caught by the emotional intensity in his dark eyes. There was no escaping the fierce passion. Did her expression reflect the same hunger his did as he gazed down at her?

Eye sex. She'd heard the phrase but never experienced it before. The look he gave her was smoldering, showing her that he found her attractive. No, more than that. Showing her that he wanted to rip her clothes off and steam up the windows by making love to her right there in the front seat of his car.

She couldn't believe he was looking at her, Heather couldn't-get-a-date-to-senior-prom Grayson, that way. It was intense, it was raw, and the unexpected delight of it made her breath catch in the back of her throat, as if she were a child making a wish on her birthday candles.

The headlights of another car pulling into the lot finally intruded on the moment, startling Heather and Jason, bringing them both back to the reality of their surroundings.

As Jason straightened up and closed the passenger door, Heather tried to regain her senses. By the time he'd joined her in the car, she'd tucked her ruined stockings and her ruined self-control out of sight.

Heather tried to act as normal as possible given the fact that she was no longer a visual virgin. She'd been ravaged in a single glance. And damn, it had felt good!

Mae West was right. It *was* better to be looked over than overlooked.

Jason didn't speak until they'd driven out of the lot and had stopped at a red light several blocks away.

"I meant to tell you that I heard part of your show this afternoon," he said, looking over at her.

"What did you think?"

"That you're good at what you do."

"Just like you." The best eye sex she'd ever had. "It seems like you have a reputation."

"For what?" he asked suspiciously.

"A number of things. Being a very good prosecutor. Being a very good saxophone player. Being one of Chicago's sexiest bachelors."

"The first statement is true. The second isn't. I'm not as good as I'd like to be. The third I keep telling you I'd rather forget," he reminded her.

"Poor baby." If they knew what the man could do with a single, long, hot look, women would really be mobbing him. Heather certainly wasn't about to share the secret.

As luck would have it, a parking space in front of her building became free just as they arrived. When Jason came around to open the passenger door for her, she'd stepped out before realizing her feet were still bare. Doing a fair imitation of someone walking on hot coals, she hopped a few steps before he took things into his own hands, literally.

Scooping her up in his arms, he gallantly carried her to her front door before she could voice a protest. Once there, he carefully set her down, letting her body slide against the entire length of his, making her very much aware of every single masculine inch.

What now? Should she invite him in? Ply him with drinks and seduce him?

No. Absolutely not. She'd made enough of a fool of herself for one night. Time to say "Good night, Gracie," and send him on his way.

Would he kiss her good-night? The anticipation was kissing...uh, killing her. This was ridiculous. Was she a wimp or a woman?

Enough was enough. Just hug the man and give him a friendly peck for the road.

"Thanks for brainstorming with me tonight, Jason." A natural-born hugger, she gave him a quick squeeze and brushed her lips across his.

Heather had meant the kiss to be teasing and fun. And it was. It was also like stars colliding, showering light and magic. His lips were warm. She hadn't expected them to be so soft, or so capable of doing such wonderfully unexpected things to her. Then Jason began adding his own seductive slant. She'd wondered if his glasses would get in the way, but they didn't.

His brief kiss at the restaurant earlier was nothing compared to this. That had been a gentle rain. *This* was a blizzard, dazzling her, whiting out her surroundings and focusing her entire existence on the contact between them. Excitement surged in her veins until her entire body was flushed with it. At Andre's she'd been too stunned to respond. Not true now.

Now she reciprocated, parting her lips and allowing him entrance as he delicately sipped at her mouth. His feathery caress on the roof of her mouth raised the stakes to a new dimension of desire. It was as if an internal switch had been thrown, flooding her with blind yearning.

The moistness of his tongue diverted her as he brushed his open mouth across her skin, gently traversing her face, her neck, the sweet hollow at the base of her throat. The spaghetti straps of her dress offered little resistance and neither did she.

A sweetly exhilarating weakness invaded her lower limbs, tempting her until she turned to capture his promise-making mouth with hers. His vows weren't verbal, they were sensual. And they spoke of more pleasure to come.

All this time his hands rested on her shoulders, only moving to tenderly brush her nape with his caressing fingertips. It was as if he didn't want an embrace to distract them from the simple and purely erotic bliss of lips locked together in a moist joining.

Their kiss took on a life of its own, blossoming into an intimate exchange of sleek tongues and throaty murmurs. Jason finally got to test his theory that her mouth was made for hours of French kissing. He was totally absorbed in his research, leaving no area unexplored. And in the end, he came to the conclusion that he'd been right.

Jason felt his control slipping, but he didn't care. He was too distracted by how incredibly smooth and soft her skin was. That first night he'd met her, he'd held open the door to the coffee shop for her and as she'd passed him by, her hair had brushed against his hand. That moment had stuck in his mind. Now he slipped his fingers into her hair, amazed by how silky the strands were. Baby-fine. Awesome. Every little thing about her was unexpectedly awesome.

Heather was amazed at how gently he touched her, yet how powerfully she reacted. He might not be holding her tightly in his arms, but he was kissing her with insatiable hunger and ardent passion. It was as if he was trying to tell her with his kisses what he couldn't say in words. What he'd told her with his eyes in the car—that he wanted her here and now and damn the consequences.

The sound of a siren's piercing wail finally registered in Heather's head. She hazily attributed it to her internal alarm warning her that she'd jumped in the deep end of the pool and she was going down for the third time.

What little common sense she had remaining belatedly came to her rescue. A week ago she hadn't even known Jason existed. She wasn't going to make love with him tonight. It was too soon for him to see her naked. In fact, anytime this century might be too soon. He was too perfect and she was too...*not* perfect.

Reluctantly pulling away, she inhaled a lungful of air in an attempt to clear her head. Only then did she realize that the siren was actually atop a Chicago police car as it whizzed by. She also realized that Jason's glasses were actually steamed up.

"Wow!" Jason whispered. His grin tugged at her heart, sorely testing her control.

"Yeah, wow," she repeated, equally dazed and still entranced. There was more at work here than just sex. This man had the ability to set her on fire. And being set on fire invariably meant that one ended up in a pile of ashes. Time to apply some brakes, some caution. Time to get this bet over with before she did something she'd regret.

Taking another deep breath, Heather said, "I think we've both had enough stimulation for one night."

"I can take it if you can." His look made it clear that he was primed and ready for more.

Her look made it clear that she was impressed but determined. "'Anything worth doing is worth doing slowly,'" she quoted.

"Ben Franklin?"

"Gypsy Rose Lee."

"I can kiss slowly."

"I noticed," she said. "I admire that in a man."

He leaned closer, as if to further demonstrate his ability, but she put a restraining hand on his chest to halt him. "This was only our second kiss. Imagine how good the next one will be. Tomorrow."

"Tomorrow?"

"Have you ever gone in-line skating?"

"No."

"I'll teach you how. Be here at noon. Good night. And thanks for rescuing me from that dessert cart."

Staring at her closed front door a second later, Jason wondered who was going to rescue him from a woman who made his control evaporate like water in the Sahara.

WHEN THE PHONE RANG at seven the next morning, Heather was so out of it she picked up her bedroom TV's remote control and tried to answer that before realizing it wasn't her cordless phone. From the foot of her bed, Maxie shifted his front paw over his eyes, growling at the interruption of his sleep.

Heather knew he was growling at the telephone, not her. She felt like growling at it, too. "Hello," she mumbled into the phone.

"Look, I don't like seven in the morning any more than you do," Nita grumbled, "but I couldn't get to sleep for wondering how it went last night. With you and the legal eagle. Was he upset about the little mishap at the restaurant?"

"Almost falling into the dessert cart and triggering general mayhem was not a *little* mishap," Heather said, stretching.

"It could have been worse. You could have ended up face first in that pie." Nita pointed out.

"Where were you?" Heather asked, trying to stifle a yawn.

"I ducked under the table. I thought he might recognize me and wonder what I was doing there."

"Wise move."

"Wise move having Jason save you."

"Maybe I should write a book about my experiences on how to snag a man," Heather reflected. "Tip number 203—have a drunk conventioneer tell the man of your dreams you want to have sex with him. Tip number 204—follow that up by taking a nosedive into the dessert cart of an upscale restaurant. Sure way to capture his attention."

"So are you ready to move on to the next step? Which, in case you've forgotten, is taking him skating. He hasn't done that before, has he? It would be just like Bud to hang us up on a technicality."

"No, he hasn't gone skating before. And he's coming over later today."

"Great! Then everything is going according to plan."

"Oh please, don't pretend that we ever had an actual plan to capture Jason's attention."

"Capturing his attention wasn't the bet, *snagging* him was, meaning you've got him in the palm of your hand."

Immediately, an erotic picture came to mind of her caressing a naked Jason, her hand closing over his velvety strength. She'd come close to that part of his anatomy several times the night before. So close...

As if sensing her X-rated thoughts, Nita said, "Maybe I should have said that snagging him means having him eating out of the palm of your hand, although *having* him in the palm of your hand would count in my book, too."

"You're bad," Heather said, laughing.

"It's why you like me so much. So let's cut to the chase here. Is this all wishful thinking or do you know what his clothes look like on your bedroom floor?"

"I'm not going to sleep with Jason because of a bet!" Heather said, cursing her voice for squeaking.

"Of course not. For one thing, I doubt you'd get much sleeping done. For another, you wouldn't have him in your bed because of the bet. He'd be there because he's gorgeous and you want him."

"Not on the first date."

"You're such a prude. You'd think the host of *Love on the Rocks* would be a little more…lenient." Nita clicked her tongue.

"There's a reason the show isn't called *Lust on the Rocks.*"

"Because you refused to let marketing change the name. But let's get back to Jason here. How soon before I can show Bud the agony of defeat?"

"I'll tell you the same thing I told Jason last night. Don't rush me."

"Rush you? Which means he wanted to land his 747 on your runway, run his diesel engine on the express tracks to your internal station." Nita gave no indication that she heard Heather's choked laughter. "That's great. You've given me renewed hope that you're going to win this bet after all. Now if I can just find that cute cab driver again, we'll all be happy."

"IF YOU WANT TO BREAK my legs, why not just do it now and get it over with?" Jason said as he struggled to hold on to the back of a park bench in order to stay upright.

Heather had brought Jason here to one of the smaller, lesser known of Chicago's famous lakefront parks because it topped her list of favorite places in the city. Especially on a postcard perfect spring day like today. "Make no little plans, they have no magic to stir men's blood," she murmured.

"Let me guess. Gypsy Rose Lee?"

"Daniel Burnham, lakefront architect." She waved

her hand toward the city skyline, all sharp angles and reflective glass, on the other side of the Outer Drive. It looked great from here. So did Jason, wearing his black jeans and T-shirt, what she liked to think of as his Dark Knight attire. The dark glasses he wore made him look like a lean and sexy Blues Brother.

Gazing back at the urban skyline, Heather fondly reflected how much she loved this view of the city. She also loved the endearing way that Jason was unable to keep his balance on the rented in-line skates. Maybe she had some sublimated need to keep him as off balance as she felt. "Are you sure you don't want to take off your sunglasses?"

"They're prescription. If I take them off I might run someone over."

"To do that, you'd have to move first," she noted wryly.

"I am moving. That's the problem."

"You're swaying in place. That's not the same thing as skating. Here, hang on to me."

Jason gingerly shifted his grip from the bench to her, wrapping both arms around her before flashing her a naughty grin. "This is much better." Now he had no trouble staying upright. In fact, he was moving like a pro, and not just at in-line skating. His hands rested on the small of her back, his outstretched fingers provocatively close to the curve of her derriere.

"You fake!" she exclaimed. "You knew how to do this all the time."

"I would have thought my kiss last night would have convinced you of that," Jason said, with a teasing smile.

"I was referring to in-line skating," Heather replied demurely.

"I haven't been in-line skating before. But I've been ice skating since I was three." He would never have agreed to this outing if he hadn't known what he was doing. Looking the fool was not on his agenda. "And I played hockey in high school," he added.

"Hockey, huh?" She gave him a speculative look. "Ever break your nose?"

"No. Why? Are you going to repay me that way?"

"I don't believe in violence. I prefer other means." Reaching under his upraised arms, she tickled his armpits.

Jason squirmed away from her with boyish outrage, his dark hair falling over his forehead. "Hey, that's no fair!"

"All's fair in love and war."

"Which of those are we talking about here?" he asked.

To which she replied, "Ice cream."

"I don't recall that being on the list of choices."

Heather pointed down the path with a smile of anticipation. "An ice-cream cart is coming this way."

"Is this another case of you eating when you're nervous?"

Instead of answering, she said, "Last one to the cart pays," before taking off in a burst of speed.

Jason lost valuable time being distracted by the tempting sway of her rounded hips displayed to the best advantage from his location behind her. The Bermuda shorts she wore were demure by most standards. That just whet his appetite all the more.

He couldn't believe how much he wanted her. Not that he was the kind of man who rushed into things. But then he wasn't the kind of man who would normally be caught dead skating along the lakeside, either. Heather had a way about her that made the unexpected appealing.

She didn't fit into his plans, but then there was room for a dalliance. And there was no one he'd rather dally with than Heather. No other woman had intrigued him to this extent. That didn't mean he was in danger of losing control of the situation, he reassured himself, squelching his inner fears. After all, he wasn't talking about love. He was talking about sex. The bottom line was that he wanted this woman in his bed.

As a result of his ogling her, Jason came in second. Obviously her motto of Anything Worth Doing Is Worth Doing Slowly didn't apply to in-line skating.

But he consoled himself with the way she melted against him when he deliberately bumped into her as a way of stopping himself, gently sandwiching her between him and the ice-cream vendor's cart. The same rounded derriere he'd been admiring earlier now fit snugly against his arousal.

"You lost," she breathlessly stated.

"The race, maybe," he whispered against her ear. "Not the war."

"I didn't realize this was a battle," she said, gulping.

"I thought your radio show specializes in the battle of the sexes," he murmured.

Leaning back against him and giving a tempting little wiggle, she flashed him a saucy look over her shoulder as she said, "Which means I've got plenty of ammunition in my arsenal, so you'd better watch out."

Placing his hand on his heart, he dramatically reeled back from her before giving her a grin as sexy as hers had been. "Thanks for the warning, but I think I'll take my chances."

"And I'll take a Chocolate Drumstick." She stepped away from him to ask, "What would you like?"

"Couldn't you tell?"

"Now that you mention it, yes, I could tell that you were...dying for something. A frozen yogurt with nuts?"

"I didn't think freezing was good for...nuts."

"You'd know that better than I," she noted demurely. "I've heard drenching them in chocolate syrup can be good."

"Sounds like that might have possibilities. Care to demonstrate?"

"Certainly. Here." She gave him the frozen treat the ice-cream vendor handed her. "That should cool you off."

"You're good at this." Jason's look made it clear that he was referring to her flirtatious comebacks.

"You're not too bad yourself."

"Thanks."

They stopped at a nearby, empty park bench to enjoy their ice cream. Once they sat down, Heather realized why it had remained empty on a busy Saturday. It was set on an incline, which meant that the person on her end of the bench ended up with their feet dangling in the air.

"You're too short on one end," Jason noted as he finished his ice cream.

"I'm not too short." Heather was defensive about her height, or lack thereof, because her sister was tall and willowy like their mom. Standing next to the pair of them, Heather had always felt like a stout stump. "The bench is on a slant. Your legs are longer than mine—you could swap seats with me."

"I happen to like your seat the way it is. Fills out a pair of shorts extremely nicely. I can think of a way of solving your height problem, however." Putting his hands beneath her legs, he draped first one, then the other across his lap. "That's better," he said with a great deal of satisfaction while she grabbed on to his shoulders to regain her balance. She was now seated at a right angle to him, her shoulder bumping against his chest, her hip nudging the placket of his jeans.

"Mmm." Jason nuzzled the nape of her neck. "You smell good."

"Balance. The name of my perfume is Balance. I don't have much of that in my life, so figured I might as well have some in my perfume."

Attempting to be nonchalant about her now provocative pose, she kept her gaze focused on the many boats on the lake, their colorful sails swelling in the cooling lake breeze. It didn't help. She needed to focus on something nonsexual. His job. She latched on to the subject like a drowning woman reaching for a lifesaver.

"So what made you want to be a prosecutor instead of a defense attorney? I'm assuming you didn't decide to work in the D.A.'s office for the prestige or the money or the glamour," she teased.

"Glamour? Right. Doing paperwork, filing cases, reading case law, that's all real glamorous. You're the one with the glamorous job, not me."

"You bet. I look real glamorous," she said, giving up the battle and swinging her legs from his lap as she rubbed a smudge of dirt off her left knee. "You're the one with your picture on the cover of magazines all over the city."

"Don't remind me. And I became a prosecutor because of the victims, because of wanting to right a wrong, see that a crime is punished." Frowning, he added, "But it doesn't always work out that way. In a trial, I can't control what the judge or jury is going to do."

"And you like being in control?"

"To be in hell is to drift. To be in heaven is to steer. So said George Bernard Shaw. And I agree. So yes, I like being in control."

As she absently finished the rest of her ice cream, Heather couldn't help wondering how she fit into his controlled plans. She had an uneasy feeling she didn't. Not in the long term. Women who wore key lime pie on their shoes weren't easy to steer. They tended to veer off in unknown directions. Did he know that?

"I've been uptight, waiting for a jury to come in with a verdict, and you've helped me relax today." He tucked a loose strand of her fiery hair behind her ear. "I owe you for that."

"You don't owe me for that. You *do* owe me for that ice cream I bought you." Her smile was sassy.

"Yes, I do. So let me thank you." Jason brushed his mouth over hers. He teased her by running his tongue along the seam of her lips until she parted them. Taking his sweet time, he explored and sampled, captivated and tantalized.

The sun beating down on her head was nothing compared to the heat he was generating deep within her. Pulling her even deeper into the kiss, he ran his tongue over the smooth enamel of her front teeth. He tasted like chocolate and other sinful temptations.

Things were just getting really interesting when they were rudely interrupted by the strident sound only a child can make. An *unhappy* child.

"You're on my bench," a little boy wearing a Michael Jordan jersey shouted at them. "No kissing on my bench!"

6

"YOU HEARD THE KID," Heather murmured against Jason's lips, her voice tinged with laughter. "No kissing on his bench."

As they got up and skated away under the disapproving eye of their pint-size chaperon, Jason muttered, "You enjoyed that, didn't you?"

"You bet. Didn't you?" she asked, blinking at him guilelessly while skating circles around him. "You were sure acting like you enjoyed it."

"I wasn't referring to the kiss. I meant embarrassing me," he said.

"It wouldn't bother you if you weren't such a stuffed shirt," she teased, yanking on his immaculately pressed T-shirt for good measure.

"Are you saying I'm too uptight and stiff?" he demanded.

"Blimey, a man can never be too stiff or too rich," Heather retorted in an audacious English accent, accompanied by a cheeky grin that faded as she remembered Nita and Bud were somewhere in the vicinity, keeping tabs on her progress. She'd forgotten all about them for a while there.

In fact, she'd forgotten about everything but Jason, and that was a dangerous thing to do. Because no matter how charming he was, no matter how incredibly well he kissed, there was no getting around the fact that he was the city's sexiest bachelor, used to having beautiful women on his arm.

Spending time with Jason was making her wish she were prettier, thinner, taller, sexier. And that wasn't a good thing. She'd been down that road before, too many times. It was strewn with potholes you could lose your self-identity in.

It had taken Heather years to accept herself for who she was. She didn't need Jason rocking the boat for her now.

Her dark thoughts were interrupted by the sight of a head bobbing behind a nearby bush. A second later the head bobbed again, the sunlight bouncing off the shiny bald spot on top. The pervert hiding in the bushes was none other than Bud. She'd recognize his tacky taste in clothes anywhere. Not to mention the smell of his cigars.

But it smelled like something more than a cigar was burning. Bud's way of hiding his smoking in their supposedly smoke-free office was to simply put the cigar behind his back, as if that made it all right. Heather had often thought it was only a matter of time before he set himself on fire.

Sure enough, a small column of smoke rose from behind him as Bud saw she was looking his way and ducked down behind the bush again. He didn't stay there long, however. A minute later, he leaped out, yelping and smacking the smoking seat of his yellow-and-green-checked golfing pants.

Immediately, everyone's eyes were on him and his strange ants-in-his-pants antics.

"What's wrong with him?" Jason asked.

"I guess he found himself in the hot seat once too often," Heather said as Bud headed straight for the lake and dunked his steaming butt in the chilly water.

"If that's the case, then I guess he's learned his lesson," Jason noted.

"I doubt it," Heather muttered, wondering where Nita was. Up a tree somewhere? This was turning into a farce.

It couldn't continue. She had to get this ridiculous bet out of the way as soon as possible. Then her life could get back to normal. She didn't need a drop-dead-gorgeous man like Jason resurrecting her long-buried fears and doubts.

"So where do we go from here?" Jason asked.

"To Navy Pier."

"I SEE NO SIGN that these two recognize they are soul mates." The declaration came from Muriel, who didn't sound the least bit pleased by the current state of affairs. She dangled her bare feet over the edge of the tree branch.

"Jason is intrigued by her," Betty stoutly maintained, straddling a nearby branch like a roughrider while ducking in time to avoid being hit by a leaf waving in the breeze.

"And she's attracted to him," Hattie added. She'd placed a velvet pillow upon the tree branch she'd chosen, not wanting the rough bark to snag her sky blue dress or mess up her hairdo. "She's just finding it difficult to believe he's the one for her."

"And I'm finding it difficult to believe that we actually *wanted* to be fairy godmothers." Muriel's ample bosom heaved with her put-upon sigh.

"It seemed like a good idea at the time."

"We don't have time for a trip down memory lane, for petunia's sake," Betty briskly reminded them. Today her T-shirt said Caution—I've Got An Attitude And I Know How To Use It.

"Those who don't learn from their mistakes are doomed to repeat them." Muriel's prophesy was delivered with a face of gloom.

Betty's aggravation increased as her wings nearly got whacked by a leaf. Hopping off the branch, she hovered in midair to put her hands on her waist and glare down at her two sisters. "Stop being such fussbudgets. I don't know what you've got your knickers in a knot about. Things are going just fine. Heather will win her bet, that beastly Bud will have to be nice to his co-workers for a year and Jason will marry Heather."

At which time, Hattie inserted her own fairy dust's worth. "Remember, these are humans we're working with. They never seem to conform to plans, even when they're babies. I've got a bad feeling about Heather winning this bet."

"Meaning she loses it?"

Hattie shook her head so vehemently that her sunflower-adorned straw hat tumbled into her eyes. "I've got a bad feeling about that, too."

"What don't you have a bad feeling about?"

Betty's increasing exasperation was evident. "I thought that's what our plan was, for her to win the bet and Jason."

"You know what they say about the best laid plans of mice and fairy godmothers..." Hattie intoned. "If she wins the bet, she may lose Jason. And if she loses the bet, she may lose her self-esteem. My instincts tell me we need to fix the Ferris wheel so that Heather won't win or lose the bet. Some bad weather should do the trick. They shut it down during storms."

Muriel had the final word. "I guess that means we punt and work on the weather until we fine-tune the details."

HEATHER AND NITA rendezvoused in the ladies' room on Navy Pier. Luckily it wasn't crowded, allowing them some privacy as they stood in front of the huge mirror along one wall. Nita was wearing a brief lime green tank top and an even briefer pair of black shorts.

"I'm getting pretty good at this charade stuff," Nita was bragging as she reapplied her cherry red lipstick.

Heather gave her an admonishing look. "I would not call crossing your legs, hopping and pointing to the bathroom a totally discreet means of communication. And don't get used to this mime stuff. You're having entirely too much fun with this."

"Oh, and you're not? Come on, I saw the two of you on that park bench, with Jason kissing you and you kissing him back. You're doing just great! You're two out of three right now. Bud is on the ropes. You're ready to give him the knockout punch.''

"Enough already with the sports analogies," Heather requested. "You've been hanging out with Bud too much."

"Any time spent with Bud is *too* much time."

After restoring some order to her hair, Heather dropped her comb back in her tiny purse. "Where is he, by the way?"

"He's here at Navy Pier. I saw him a few minutes ago wearing an I Love Chicago T-shirt pulled down to his knees to cover the burn marks on the seat of his pants."

"He didn't hurt himself, did he?" Heather asked, feeling guilty.

"Just his pride, which he has too much of anyway."

"I can't believe I'm doing this." Shaking her head, Heather gazed at her reflection in the mirror as if searching for answers. "I should never have let you and Bud rope me into this. I'd never advise one of my callers to do what I'm doing."

Nita patted Heather's shoulder reassuringly. "What they don't know won't hurt them."

"What about Jason?"

"What he doesn't know won't hurt him, either."

"But *I* know. And I feel badly about it."

"Feel badly about it later," Nita ordered briskly. "For now, listen while I coach you on making out on a Ferris wheel. The trick is not to get sick on the darn thing. You don't, do you?"

"I don't know. I've never ridden one."

"So this is your maiden voyage, huh? That's great. Then you don't even have to fake the fear and panic."

Heather winced. "Gee, you make it sound so appealing."

"Just hang on to Jason as if he was saving your life."

"You sound like my mother." At Nita's affronted glare, Heather said, "Well, you do. She used to tell me to act meek and helpless and maybe some boy would feel sorry enough for me to take me out."

"Well, that's the difference between me and your mom. One of them, anyway. I'm not saying to act mild or helpless. I'm talking about physical contact here."

But Heather had had her fill of advice. "Forget it. I'm just going to get on the ride and see what happens."

"Fine. Bud and I will stay down here and observe you."

"Wait a minute." Heather grabbed Nita's arm. "I saw the promo on this ride. The Ferris wheel is fifteen stories high! Neither of you would be able to tell what was going on if you stay down here. Why aren't you going on the ride?" she added suspiciously.

"Number one, because we're afraid of heights. Number two, because if we sit close enough to watch you, then Jason would be able to see us. And he'd get suspicious."

"You and Bud could pretend to be dating," Heather suggested.

"Bite your tongue!"

As she and Jason stood in line to get on the Ferris wheel, Heather was silently making excuses for her mixed emotions about him. Nita had been right about one thing: Heather *was* having fun with Jason. Too much fun. Enough fun to make her nervous.

Maybe she was feeling so jittery because it had been a while since she'd had a date. She put in long hours at the station and didn't have much time or energy to devote to her private life. Not that she'd had much of a private life since Howard had taken off to commune with ferns.

Sure, plenty of men were attracted to her radio personality, and Heather got piles of fan mail from men wanting to meet her. Or, rather, they wanted to meet the woman she sounded like, not the woman she was.

If you look half as good as you sound, you must be really hot. That line showed up in a lot of the letters Heather received from her male audience.

That fact was brought home to her whenever she was out and about and someone recognized her name, or her voice. They'd look at her as if she'd been trapped in the wrong body. It was a look she'd gotten all too often from her own parents, and she didn't need to be getting it from strangers as well.

Jason, however, didn't look at her that way. But one afternoon of in-line skating did not a relationship make. She wanted the man in her life to make her feel good about herself, not make her doubt herself even more than usual.

"Let me do it, let me do it!" Hattie was imploring Betty. "I never get to play with weather magic."

"What about that freak tornado in Nebraska?"

"Nebraska gets plenty of tornadoes."

"Not in January." Betty retorted. "You're just lucky I fixed it as fast as I did."

"So I got a little overzealous. Like you've never gotten overzealous? What about the time—"

Betty cut her off by putting her hand over Hattie's mouth. "All right already. You can do the weather magic. All we need is enough rain and lightning to shut down the ride. Nothing more. So be careful."

HEATHER HAD HEARD the phrase "the heavens opened," but she'd never been standing under them when it happened. The dark rain clouds blew in off the lake without any warning, scattering the crowd, who hadn't expected any precipitation since the skies had been clear a short while before.

The Ferris wheel closed for business because of the weather. Heather knew a cosmic hint when she got one. She was ready to call it quits for the day.

As Jason drove her home, she prepared herself to be calm and collected when or if he kissed her. She opened her front door and turned to say something, and his lips brushed hers.

Rational thought went out the window. She and Jason ended up on her couch, she wasn't sure how. She was too busy being kissed, gently, rapidly, successively. There and gone, there and gone, until she reached both hands around his head and held his teasing mouth in place atop hers.

Jason deepened the kiss without hurrying it. Timeless kisses. Inventive kisses. Slowly tasting the inner curve of her lower lip with his tongue, he reverently paid tribute to her mouth, treating it as if it were a warm subterranean temple with arched ceilings. The delicate yet torrid caress on the roof of her mouth made her shiver with desire.

It was as if she'd never been kissed before, as if she were discovering the process for the very first time. He caressed her with soul-stealing longing, using his lips, tongue and teeth to express every nuance of need and passion.

The circle of his arms grew smaller as he molded her more tightly against him on the welcoming softness of the couch. Pressed against him from shoulder to thigh, her body hummed with anticipation. The thin cotton of her shorts provided no protection from the hard ridge of his desire.

Bending her knee, she cradled him against her. She could feel the muscles of his thighs flexing against hers as he shifted against her, causing her to gasp in undisguised passion.

The expression of Heather's pleasure was Jason's reward for his leisurely, intimate movements. He remembered Heather telling him that nothing worth doing wasn't worth doing slowly. So he'd deliberately paced himself. Knowing his intense arousal put him in a time warp that turned one minute into ten, he repeated every movement, telling himself he had all night to explore every inch of her mouth, and her body.

Moving too fast meant he might miss something, like the delicious hollow at the base of her throat. She tasted like strawberries as he licked his way to the open V-neck of her T-shirt. Nudging aside the warm cotton, he nuzzled the shadowy hollow between her breasts.

He could feel her response as her full breasts thrust softly against his chest, her nipples urging him to visit them next. But he took his time, lifting her T-shirt until he felt the beat of her heart against his open mouth. There he lingered until he'd undone the front fastener of her bra.

Now there was nothing to interfere with his erotic travels. Stroking the underside of her breasts with the tips of his fingers, he directed the rest of his attention to kissing each creamy rise, leisurely ascending all the way to the rosy tips. Once there he staked his claim, wetting her with his tongue before blowing gently on her skin.

He took his time to suckle and tease, brush and graze, until she was utterly steeped in passion. He discovered that a flick of his curled tongue applied just so made her purr.

Heather was in heaven, driven there by a devilish angel who taught her what it felt like to be truly adored. She slid her fingers through Jason's hair as he bent his head yet again. How much more of this could she take? She was already damp between her legs.

As if to answer her unspoken question, he slid his hand beneath the wide cuff of her shorts and up her thigh to the heart of her femininity. He teased her there, too, exploring without hurrying, advancing and retreating.

His finger stole beneath the elastic of her silky

panties to brush against her hidden curls. His touch was just like his kisses, there and gone, there and gone, there…there…lingering, gliding, sliding, closer…closer…until he parted the soft folds between her legs to stroke her inside and out. His skilful fingers practiced their blissful magic while his sexy mouth surrounded her breast. Jason lavished her with attention, with tiny thrusts and provocative swirls.

The tension spiraled, thrusting her into a world of suspended anticipation of almost unbearable pleasure. Crossing her legs only trapped his hand more intimately against her. One brush of his thumb against the tiny nub hidden in her crisp curls and she was a goner. Her orgasm took her, showering over her, expanding and contracting until she was flooded with sensual fulfilment.

Jason thought he'd never heard such a wonderful sound as her voice, rich with satisfaction, murmuring his name. Looking down at her, he gently smoothed her hair away from her face. "From the first moment I saw you, I knew you were different. So open and honest."

Open and honest. The words echoed in her head with mocking repetition. Open and honest. Not true. Sex and lies. A dangerous combination.

Even more dangerous was the fact that Heather now knew this was more than just sex. She'd never let another man do what Jason had just done. She'd never shared that much of herself, left herself that vulnerable. Love. Passion. Infatuation. She was in way over her head here.

What had ever made her think she could manage a

mixed-up mess like this? Her love life had been rocky before, but nothing like this. She had no experience with this kind of blind panic. Jason had a way of touching her soul that scared her spitless. If he knew the truth, if he found out about the damn bet, he'd hate her. She knew it. She had to stop this before the pain became something she'd never be able to recover from.

"If there's one thing I hate it's lies," Jason was saying, hammering more nails in her emotional coffin. "But enough talking. Where were we...?" He leaned down to kiss her again.

"You were just leaving!" Heather declared, frantically pushing him away.

7

"Ouch!" Jason yelped, landing on the floor with a thump. "What the hell did you do that for?"

"You've got to leave now," Heather repeated, smoothing out her mussed clothing with frenzied fingers.

"Leave?" Jason repeated in confusion. "You're kidding, right?"

"No." She leaped from the couch as if it were an instrument of the devil.

Things had gotten completely out of control. And she'd let them. She'd allowed herself to be carried away in the tidal wave of grand passion. And more.

She'd fallen in love with Jason Knight. A man who valued honesty. A man who had zero tolerance for lies. A man who didn't approve of betting and hated surprises. A man who thought she'd been honest with him. A man who knew nothing about the incriminating bet she'd entered into with Bud.

There was no way upstanding, honorable Jason would understand that she'd tried to snag him to prove a point. God! She wished she'd never heard of the word snag, and wished more than ever that she'd just blown Bud off when he'd baited her into agreeing to the bet.

Instead she was the one who'd learned a painful lesson. Bets and romance didn't mix.

Jason sat on the floor and eyed her warily. "What's wrong?"

"I can't do this. I think it would be best if we didn't see each other anymore."

"Is this some kind of sick joke?" he demanded, running an impatient hand through his dark hair before getting to his feet with catlike grace. "A minute ago you were with me all the way. Are you saying that I imagined your response to me? That you were an unwilling participant?"

"No." She looked away. "I'm sorry. I can't explain."

"Try."

Heather couldn't try. She was too concerned with trying not to cry in front of him to be able to explain things to him. Besides, explaining meant telling him the truth and she couldn't do that. Call her a coward, but at that moment she couldn't bear to see the censure in his eyes. So she said the thing that would get rid of him the fastest. "I'm in love with someone else."

Sure enough, two minutes later Jason was gone. He didn't even slam her front door. Instead he closed it with controlled emphasis.

"CALL BACK LATER," Nita mumbled into the phone.

"Don't hang up!" Heather yelled, sitting up in her bed. "I need your help."

"Do you know what time it is?"

Heather glanced at her clock. "It's seven in the morning."

"On a Sunday. My day off," Nita groaned.

"You called me yesterday morning at seven," Heather said defensively.

"So what is this, payback time?"

"No, it's panic time."

"I don't like the sound of that," Nita grumbled. "This sounds like something I'd understand better with some caffeine in my system. Hang on while I switch to my cordless phone. Okay, I'm heading toward the kitchen. I've got the coffee machine turned on. Until it starts perking, you better start at the beginning and speak slowly and clearly. Remember, you are speaking to someone who is just about comatose."

"It's all over," Heather tragically declared.

"That's the beginning?"

"The end."

"I said to start at the beginning."

"I'm not going to see Jason anymore. This entire situation has gotten way out of hand. I should never have agreed to this ridiculous wager in the first place. I must have been temporarily insane." Trying to stay calm, Heather leaned back against the pile of pillows she'd stuffed behind her.

"I don't think that defense is going to stand up in court," Nita said matter-of-factly.

"Don't mention courts. It makes me think of Jason."

"Forget starting at the beginning," Nita decided. "Skip to the chase. What's the bottom line here?"

"I'm calling the bet off." Heather's voice rose as panic took hold.

"You can't do that. If you do, you'll lose."

"I don't care," Heather said grimly.

"Easy for you to say, you don't have five hundred dollars resting on this!"

"You shouldn't have bet that much if you couldn't afford to lose it."

"What are you, a representative of Gamblers Anonymous?" Nita retorted in exasperation. "I'm telling you, you can't quit. The women of WMAX are counting on you. Do you know what kind of hell Bud will make of our lives if you give in now? We'll never hear the end of it. And that's not all. He'll start rumors about how the show host of Chicago's most popular relationship talk show can't even handle her own romantic relationships. I'm telling you, there's no going back now."

"Nita, listen to me." Heather's voice was becoming increasingly more frantic. "I can't do this anymore."

"Something happened last night. What was it? Jason didn't attack you or anything, did he?"

"No. If there was any attacking going on I did it."

"Was he protesting?" Nita asked.

"No."

"Then it wasn't an attack, it was a seduction."

It had been that, all right. And so much more. He'd stolen her heart. "It's not a game anymore. This has gotten serious. I think I'm falling for this guy."

"And what's wrong with that?"

"Everything," Heather wailed. "Do you know

what he told me was one of the things he admired most about me? My honesty. That I've always been upfront and straight with him.''

"Uh-oh. You didn't tell him about the bet, did you?"

"No. Don't you see? I've been deceiving him from the very beginning."

"So wait a few months—or better yet, years—and then tell him. It will be something the two of you will be able to laugh about with your kids and grandkids.''

"I thought I could keep things under control, but I'm way out of my league here. I'm in over my head.''

"Okay, okay, I get the idea." Nita said. "Just calm down and tell me what happened in the past twenty-four hours to change things. Yesterday you were handling the situation just fine.''

"Jason and I made out on my couch. Big-time."

"And that was a problem?"

"I liked it."

"That's good to hear." Nita stated with wry humor.

"Too much."

"Trust me, you can't like making out too much."

"You can when your heart is in jeopardy."

"So what did you do?" Nita demanded.

"I told him I couldn't see him again. And I told him another lie—that I was in love with someone else. To cover my first lie, I had to tell a second. I thought it wouldn't hurt, but it does. It hurts so damn much."

Somehow Nita was able to follow her disjointed

rambling. "Aw jeez, you do have it bad. Falling for him wasn't part of the plan, kiddo."

"Don't you think I know that?" Heather shot back.

"You're sure it's not just a case of raging hormones? I mean, you haven't known the guy all that long."

"You know how I tease callers about love at first sight?"

"Yeah."

"Well, the joke is on me this time, and I'm not laughing anymore." In fact, she was on the verge of tears, her voice cracking with the strain.

Nita's voice softened. "You don't think he'd understand if you explained the bet to him?"

"No. Trust me, he would not be amused. I know enough about his character type to know that. And he'd find out, I know he would. I didn't have any other choice. I had to stop things from going any further before any more damage was done."

"But if this guy is the one for you..." For the first time, Nita sounded uncertain.

Heather wanted to yank the covers over her head and weep. "Maybe it is just raging hormones, after all."

"And maybe the earth is flat. I don't think so."

Heather sighed. "Me, either."

"YOU'RE LISTENING to *Love on the Rocks* and we're talking to Annie from Aurora this afternoon. Go ahead, Annie."

"There's this guy who lives in the same building I do. I knew the first time I saw him in the elevator that he was the one for me. I know you don't believe in love at first sight..."

Heather shot a killer look at Nita through the booth window. If Monday's weren't already hard enough to deal with, now she had Nita tweaking her broken heart. "Well, actually, Annie, I've had a change of heart on that subject. I'm now willing to admit that love at first sight might exist, after all. So you fell for this guy the first time you saw him. Your toes curled and your heart actually did take a flip or two." Heather certainly knew how that felt. "What's the problem?"

"Do you think it's really love I feel for him?"

"Only you can know that for sure. Tell me how he makes you feel," Heather asked, while typing on her computer link, *You're dead meat, Nita!*

Heather listened to the caller's comments with one part of her, while the other part reflected on the fact that Nita had chosen this call deliberately, hoping to make Heather change her mind about seeing Jason again and not cancelling the bet.

After Annie had waxed eloquently about how her loved one made her feel, Heather had to silently admit that she and Annie shared the same symptoms.

"Sounds to me like you love him, Annie," she said when the woman paused for breath.

"I'm scared because there's something I haven't told him. About myself, I mean," Annie said, her voice trembling.

"What haven't you told him?"

"That I'm really a man."

Heather recovered quickly enough to hit the so-low-it's-in-the-basement deep-pitched-voice tape, the one that exclaimed "Oh, no!" whenever she needed it, before wryly noting, "Well, you might have a problem there, Annie. But as I was trying to explain to a dense friend just the other day—" Heather gave Nita a meaningful glare "—the truth is bound to come out, sooner or later. So good luck to you and your Prince Charming, Annie."

Once they'd made the break to commercials, Heather stuck her tongue out at Nita, who opened the adjoining door to pop into the studio.

"I didn't know Annie used to be a man, I swear. I hope you won't hold that against me," Nita added before making another pitch to save the bet.

Heather cut her off. "Forget it."

"Think of all I've done for you," Nita said.

"I am thinking. Of Omar. Of you at the restaurant right before I ran into that waiter." Heather tapped her fingernails on the console.

For once, Nita was speechless. She simply shrugged and returned to the production booth.

Once Nita was gone, Heather leaned into the mike and adjusted the slide volume control on the console. "And we're back with—" she checked the computer screen ahead of her "—Bob from Burbank. What can we do for you, Bob?"

"A few minutes ago you were talking about the truth coming out. And I was wondering, how important is honesty in a relationship?"

"Depends what you're talking about. If she asks you if she really looks fat in a certain dress, then honesty may not be the best course of action. If she asks you if you're seeing another woman, then we're talking about something else again.''

"So you're saying honesty isn't necessarily important?''

"If you're not afraid of the truth, then you have nothing to worry about.''

But Heather was afraid of the truth. She was also afraid of having fallen in love with a man who loved control in his life and hated lies and surprises.

"What about private investigators?'' Bob asked. "Do you think it's fair for a woman to hire one to check up on me—I mean, to check up on a guy? Isn't that entrapment or something?''

Heather quickly activated the slide on a sound effect she hadn't used for a while, the *thump, thump, thump* of footsteps approaching. "If you've got nothing to hide, then investigating you won't reveal anything, aside from the fact that you and your significant other have a problem with trust. You might want to talk to her about that issue, Bob. Thanks for calling.'' She punched the next phone line. "Go ahead, Sue from Streamwood.''

"I was just wondering why men are so sensitive about criticism from a woman. I don't want to hurt his feelings, but each time we go out he acts like such a jerk that I could die.''

"Don't die, Sue. We need all the callers we can get. Tell me, what kind of things does he do?''

"He gets real huffy if I try and correct his bad manners. He says I should accept him and appreciate him and I shouldn't be so disapproving.''

"Well, some experts say men act this way regarding criticism from the women they care about because it makes them insecure. Try telling him how sexy you find guys who have good manners and see where that gets you, Sue. And next we have Val from Vernon Hills. You're on the air.''

''Yeah, well, your earlier caller was talking about private investigators. I'm having my boyfriend investigated and I was wondering if he's going to be upset. I mean, what if he finds out?''

''What made you hire an investigator?''

''My boyfriend would disappear for a week at a time and not tell me where he was. At first I tried to check him out myself by getting this book, *Be Your Own Dick.* But my boyfriend saw the cover and thought it was some kind of perverted sex-therapy book.'' Through the booth window, Heather watched as Miguel choked on his coffee. ''I got it away from him before he could check it out. But then I hired a professional.''

''Good luck, Val, and what can I say?'' This time Heather chose the sound of a gong. ''Sometimes these things are best left to the professionals. That wraps up today's version of *Love on the Rocks,* where we keep those relationships stirred, not shaken.''

Miguel, still wiping tears of mirth from his face, added their sign-off of ice cubes hitting the sides of a glass.

Taking off her headset, Heather leaned forward to rest her forehead against the edge of the console table. Talk about a wild afternoon! And she had yet to speak to Bud.

She considered banging her head against the table,

but opted for sitting up and gathering her pile of notes and articles on relationships. If there weren't enough callers, she always wanted to be prepared to discuss some element of romantic relationships, and there were new books or articles being written daily. A lack of callers hadn't been the problem today.

The problem today was calling off the bet. The sooner the better. She had to reach Bud before his show started an hour from now. She found him in the break room, where he was making a mess of a Reuben sandwich in between puffs on his stogey.

"Bud, this is a smoke-free building," she reminded him, squinting and wrinkling her nose.

"Go tell it to the exhaust police," Bud replied, laughing at his own joke. "You think you're the only one who knows how to be funny? Hah!"

Waving her hand in front of her face to ward off the stink of his cigar, she reluctantly sat at the table with him. "We need to talk, Bud. About the bet."

"What about it?" His voice was muffled because he had almost half of the Reuben sandwich in his mouth.

"I think we should call it off."

"You mean you're admitting you lost?"

"No, I'm not admitting I lost. I'm saying we should call it a draw and end the bet now. It was stupid to begin with."

Nita must have spread the word about what Heather was planning to do, because within another minute the break room was filled with people—Linda, Connie, Miguel and many others. What Heather had hoped would be a private discussion showed signs of turning into a *High Noon* shootout.

"Stupid," Bud exclaimed. "Hah! If it was so stupid why did all these people put good money on the wager?"

"I'm not going to argue with you, Bud."

"That'll be a first for a woman."

"Come on, just let me have one crack at him," Nita begged from the sidelines.

"If you didn't snag Jason Knight, you lose and I win. It's as simple as that." Bud puffed out his chest. "You girls need to learn how to accept defeat like a man instead of acting like a bunch of whining broads."

He waved his cigar at Heather and crowed. "You a specialist on romance? Come on! You don't know the first thing about men. I can tell you why you lost this bet. Because when it came right down to it, you weren't woman enough to put out."

"Oh, I can put out, all right." Taking his putrid cigar out of his hand, Heather extinguished it in his coffee mug. "There. That's put out. As I said before, this is a smoke-free building."

"What's going on in here?" Bev asked as she entered the room.

"We were just discussing the fact that a certain bet is being called a draw and everyone's money will be returned to them," Heather replied.

"Sounds like a good idea to me," Bev agreed.

"That's because you were losing," Nita muttered.

"Shush," Heather whispered from beside her. "You've still got everyone's money, right?"

"Well, there was this great sale at Nordstroms...." Seeing the panicked look on Heather's face, Nita quickly added, "I was only kidding. I've got the money. You guys will take a check, right?"

"I want cash," Bud stated.

"Fine. I'll go to the ATM downstairs."

"With a group of us. I wouldn't want you welching on a bet by taking off." He glared at Nita.

"I'm not the welcher, you are," Nita retorted.

Bud smirked at her. "Liar, liar, pants on fire."

"Speaking of pants on fire, how was that dip in the lake, Bud? I didn't think the beaches officially opened until Memorial Day."

Nita and Bud were still arguing as they left the room, with most of the rest of the staff trailing behind them like lemmings.

"I'm glad to see that everyone is taking this so well," Bev noted wryly as she watched them go.

"I wasn't trying to cause trouble," Heather said, feeling miserable. This was all her fault. If she hadn't agreed to that stupid bet none of this would have happened. She would never have met Jason, would never have fallen for him. She was already missing him terribly after only one day.

Bev patted her shoulder. "I know you weren't trying to cause trouble. No hard feelings about my betting on Bud, right?"

"No hard feelings," Heather agreed. Her feelings were all reserved for Jason, and they showed no signs of abating. But she was determined to overcome them.

"I THOUGHT YOU SAID everything was under control with these two." Wrapping her arms across her ample bosom, Muriel added a disapproving sniff for good measure as she sat atop the fridge in the corner of the conference room.

"It would be under control if either of them had the sense God gave a goose," Betty irritably retorted from beside her.

"It's the *common* sense a *godmother* gave a *triplet baby*. And you're the one who gave Jason too much," Hattie noted while rearranging the pillbox hat she wore.

Betty looked like she wanted to clunk her sister with her magic wand. "That had nothing to do with them breaking up, Miss Smarty-pants. Heather is the one messing up my plans. How could I know that she'd get a fit of conscience?"

"It's not Heather's fault we made her accept that bet," Hattie said in her defense. "Or that we made that cab stop in front of Jason's nightclub."

"It's a jazz club," Muriel impatiently reminded her.

"And then we interfered again with the rain..."

"Rain?" Muriel interjected. "That was a monsoon! Half a dozen waterspouts sprang up on the lake before I got them under control."

"You're just jealous because I got to do the weather magic and you didn't," Hattie retorted.

Now Betty looked like she wanted to clobber both her squabbling sisters. "This bickering isn't getting us anywhere. We need to focus on what we're going to do next."

"You don't think we've done enough already?" Hattie nervously fingered the tiers of organdy ruffles on her lemon yellow dress while nibbling on the tip of her color-coordinated magic wand. "You know we're not supposed to interfere."

"Uniting someone with their soul mate is sure tougher than it sounds," Betty stated irritably.

"So is being fairy godmothers to triplets." Reaching inside the largest of the many pockets in her photographer's vest, Muriel pulled out an issue of *USA Today*. "This article says that there's a boom in triplet births, like we didn't know this already? I haven't gotten a full night's sleep in decades."

Ignoring her, Betty said, "I'll give them a week. If they don't come to their senses by then, I'll just have to step in."

"Oh, my stars!" Hattie nervously nibbled once more on her magic wand, leaving teeth marks this time. "We're not supposed to do that. I mean, making it rain is one thing, but what about the rules?"

Betty shrugged. "Rules were made to be broken."

"We've already broken everything else," Muriel acknowledged while smothering a tired yawn. "I suppose we might as well add rules to the list."

JASON DIDN'T EAT at this restaurant very often because it was too far from the courthouse. But he'd gotten an urgent call to meet the district attorney here, so he'd come.

Maybe this was about his promotion. Despite the momentary distraction of that wild woman with the lettered eyelids and hair in the courtroom, Jason had gone on to make a convincing and succinct closing argument. The jury had finally come back with a guilty verdict.

Thinking about distractions naturally got Jason thinking about Heather. He could have sworn that she was as honest as the day was long. And he was sure she'd wanted him. Why else would she have responded to him the way she had? Her response didn't indicate she wanted someone else. Was she on the rebound?

He wasn't the kind of man to waste time daydreaming about a woman. He was too practical for that. When he wanted a woman, she was usually his for the taking.

But there was nothing ordinary about Heather. At first glance there was nothing special about her. But her voice had made him take a second glance that first time they'd met at Muddy's. And he'd liked what he saw.

His previous relationships had been tidy and convenient. Not wild and passionate. He wasn't accustomed to dealing with women who ended up ankle-deep in key lime pie and tried to take him on a Ferris wheel ride. Heather's joy for life made him wonder what he'd been missing all these years.

He knew he was already missing her. And he wanted her back, wanted her more than ever. She'd been like a breath of fresh air in his orderly life.

When he heard her voice, he thought it was coming from a radio somewhere. Then he realized it was coming from the other side of the tall planter separating his booth from the next. Her agitated voice carried through the thick proliferation of leaves.

"I told you that bet was a bad idea," Heather was saying.

Another woman replied, "You could have won that bet and snagged Chicago's Sexiest Bachelor if you hadn't gotten cold feet."

Snagged? Jason felt the icy chill of anger envelop him as the blood froze in his veins. Someone had bet Heather that she couldn't snag the city's sexiest bachelor? He remembered her asking him about how he felt about betting. He hadn't thought anything about it at the time, but now...

"You already accomplished steps one and two, dinner out and in-line skating," the woman continued. "The only thing you had left to do was making out on the Ferris wheel, and you were on the verge of doing that when that rainstorm hit and shut everything down."

Jason remembered all too clearly Heather's insistence that they head over to Navy Pier and the Ferris wheel. He'd thought it an example of her spontaneous nature. Instead it was an example of her deviousness.

All this time he'd been thinking that Heather was different from the women who saw him as a hunk of raw meat. He thought she had something to teach him about life. Oh, she'd taught him, all right—that he was an idiot and that she was a liar. It wasn't a lesson he was about to forget. Or forgive.

"Instead you and Jason go back to your place and make out on your couch, which may have been great for you, but it didn't mean diddly-squat as far as the bet was concerned,'' the other woman was saying.

Jason couldn't stomach anymore. He'd been set up, in more ways than one. Had Heather laughed when she'd talked to her cohort about the intimate details of what had taken place on her couch?

Another thought occurred to him. Did Heather have something to do with him being at this restaurant? Had she wanted him to hear her bragging about snagging him to her sister in crime?

The only reason Jason was here was because he'd gotten a message on his voice mail supposedly from the D.A. with a request to meet him here for lunch. Only his boss never showed. Now he knew why.

Had he been a betting man, he would have bet that the D.A. had never made that call. But Jason wasn't a betting man. And he wasn't a man who forgave deception easily. He hated being made a fool of. Hated it with an intensity caused by years of being the butt of his brother Ryan's practical jokes.

Tossing enough bills on the table to cover his check he stalked out of the restaurant. Instead of a business lunch he'd ended up getting an unpalatable helping of reality.

The second shoe dropped when he got home later that night to find his father waiting for him...with an overnight bag beside him.

8

JASON WARILY EYED his dad and the incriminating suitcase. "Hey, what's up?"

"Your mother and I had a fight."

Jason swore under his breath as he belatedly recalled that he'd forgotten to speak to his father, as he'd promised Anastasia he would.

His father had gained some weight since retiring from the Chicago Transit Authority a few months back, and his thick hair was now entirely white, but Tom Knight was still a formidable figure of a man. As a kid, Jason had thought his dad looked just like a picture of Zeus he'd seen in a book at the library. Tom also had a great hook shot and a belly laugh to rival Santa's, but he wasn't laughing at the moment. "You don't mind if I stay here tonight, do you?" his dad continued, shoving up the sleeves of his Chicago Bulls sweatshirt.

"Sure. I mean no, I don't mind. Sure you can stay. Uh..." Jason didn't know what to say. His parents argued, but never to this extreme before, never to the point of having an overnight bag packed. Although he'd never felt comfortable discussing emotional issues with his father, he felt he had to make the offer. "You want to talk about it?"

"No."

Relief shot through Jason. He wanted to help his dad but with the way his luck was running lately, he'd no doubt just screw things up even more. "Okay." Opening the door to the loft, Jason ushered his father in ahead of him. "Did you eat dinner?"

"Not yet, no." Tom dropped to the couch with a sigh, wincing when it didn't give way with the same softness as his favorite recliner at home. Jason had offered to buy him a new chair, but his dad had refused, saying there was plenty of life left in the old one yet. He'd said the same thing when Jason had offered to buy his parents a condo.

"You want Chinese or pizza?"

"Chinese, but nothing too spicy. Heartburn, you know."

Jason nodded and reached for the phone book he'd left on the coffee table. "Right."

"Not that your mother helped my digestion any by siding with that woman on the radio."

Jason stopped in his tracks, the phone book dangling from his hands. "What woman?"

"That *Love on the Rocks* woman. She said men don't communicate."

Jason frowned, trying to keep up with his dad's rambling story. "Mom said that?"

"No, the radio woman did, but your mother agreed with her. Said I never talk to her. Things escalated from there. You know your mother. She's got a temper."

"Yes, but she's never kicked you out before."

"She didn't kick me out," his dad denied indignantly. "I just said I wanted some peace and quiet to watch the Bulls game. Told her I'd come here to watch it with you. Then she said 'While you're there you might as well stay the night because I don't want you coming back here and grunting at me.' Grunting. Can you believe it? She claims I sound like that guy from the movies."

"Billy Bob Thornton?"

His dad scowled at him. "How did you know which actor I meant? Has your mother been talking to you about me?"

"No." Jason knew the actor's name because he'd noted the similarities, too, as far as grunting went. Even so, that was no reason for his mom to react the way she had, and she probably wouldn't have reacted that way if Heather hadn't gotten her all riled up.

Heather had a way of stirring up trouble. The woman should be banned from the airwaves. And she should be banned from public restaurants as well. Disasters seemed to follow her like night followed day. She'd waltzed into his life and created havoc. She'd made a fool out of him. She'd kissed him with a mind-blowing passion that totally rattled him and then tossed him out on his ear with a pile of lies.

Enough was enough. It was time to turn the tables on her for a change, see how she liked having her life turned upside down. Time for him to use this supposed sex appeal of his to regain control of the situation—and make Heather rue the day she'd ever decided to try and "snag" him.

"OOPS, HATTIE MURMURED as she perched on top of Jason's entertainment center.

"I don't believe this!" Muriel was pacing across the track lighting fastened on the wall. "We turn our backs for one second and this happens."

"Well, we can't be expected to watch over them every moment of the day. I mean, we do have other triplets that need our attention."

Betty, who was slumped over a chrome piece of sculpture that matched her dejected demeanor, spoke for the first time. "I thought it was so clever to arrange it so Jason and Heather would both appear at the restaurant. I thought they'd see each other and come to their senses. How was I to know that Heather would take it into her head to drag Nita along at the last second? Or that the two of them would then blab about the bet?"

"It was clever," Hattie reassured her. "But I do confess to being concerned about this thirst for revenge Jason has. What are you doing, Muriel?"

"Counting the days until our retirement." She used her magic wand to flip through the calendar pages too fast for even a fairy godmother to see. "Only 2,643 months to go. I can't wait."

JASON WAS WAITING for Heather in the foyer of the building housing WMAX's offices the next evening. He saw her get out of the elevator. The only problem was that she wasn't alone. She was talking to a taller, older and louder woman. He remembered her now. She'd been with Heather at Muddy's.

Deciding to bide his time, Jason followed them across the foyer, waiting for the right moment to break in. Hoping to get some idea of Heather's state of mind, he began eavesdropping on them.

"I've only had one," Heather was saying.

"I think that's the safest thing to do these days," Nita agreed.

"But it's hard to keep that kind of commitment sometimes. Life gets so hectic, and there are temptations."

"Tell me about it. And as time goes on, it gets worse. You start thinking maybe it won't matter if you stray just a little."

"You start with a quickie lube job," Heather said.

Jason almost swallowed his tongue.

"And that felt so good that you stray more and more," she continued.

At which point Jason, totally distracted by now, did something he'd never done before.

THE SOUND OF A BRIEFCASE hitting the marble floor of the foyer created a noise that could be heard from one end of the building to the other. Turning to see what was going on, Heather noticed a man in a dark suit bending down to retrieve his briefcase.

"Nice butt," Nita declared, incorrigible as ever.

Heather had to agree. Did the fact that she could appreciate the build of another man mean she was getting over Jason? She had one second of hope before realizing it *was* Jason she was staring at. And he was standing only a few feet from her.

She'd hoped that every day she went without seeing him was a day she'd increased her resistance to him. But he had only to show up to blow that theory out of the water. His impact on her was a powerful as ever. Even more so, because now her heart was involved, not just her hormones.

"What are you doing here?" Heather demanded.

Jason was unable to answer that question. He was still stunned by the conversation he'd overheard Heather having with the other woman. Did women really talk about their lovers this way?

Jason decided the direct approach was called for. "I couldn't help overhearing what you two were talking about a moment ago. What *were* you talking about?"

"Not that it's any of your business, but we were talking about car mechanics," Heather tried to say nonchalantly, but she was anything but nonchalant at the unexpected pleasure of seeing Jason again. *Stay cool,* she told herself. The body, however, ignored her.

"You're seeing a car mechanic?"

"I'm going after work, yes. Why?"

"No reason. Is he the one? The *someone else* you said you were in love with?" Jason asked, anger tinging his voice despite himself.

"Oh, this is ridiculous," Nita interrupted impatiently. "She's taking her car in for a tune-up, not her body. She's not in love with anyone else. She loves—"

"Nita!" Heather wailed.

"Her job," Nita substituted.

So Heather had lied to him about being in love with someone else. That came as no surprise to Jason. After all, she'd been lying from the moment he'd met her. He still didn't know *how* Heather had tracked him down to Muddy's, but he did know *why* she'd done it—because of the damn bet.

He'd thought she was different from the other women who'd chased after him. No, she hadn't chased *him*, she'd chased the city's sexiest bachelor. It didn't matter to her who that was.

Which made him even more intent on exacting his revenge.

Jason hated being made a fool of—anyone in his family could have told Heather that. His brother, Ryan, was an inveterate practical joker. Growing up, Jason had been the butt of more than a lifetime's worth of pranks. He hated being conned above all else, besides being lied to. Heather had committed both cardinal sins.

Well, she might specialize in talk, but his specialty was persuasion. It was one of the things that made him such a good prosecutor. And he'd persuade her right into his trap, teaching her a lesson she'd never forget.

"Heather is really pretty old-fashioned about most things," Nita was telling him. "Doesn't go all the way on the first date, that kind of thing."

"I'm leaving now," Heather stated. "I refuse to stand here while you two dissect me." Pivoting on her heel, she strode off.

"Well, that went pretty well," Nita congratulated Jason, giving him a hearty pat on the back. "I'm glad you decided to come after her. Heather is one in a million. You might like knowing that her favorite chocolates are Godiva's and her favorite flowers are

Double Delight roses. The florist in this building carries them both.''

"I heard that," Heather shouted from across the lobby.

"I meant you to!" Nita shouted back.

THE FLOWERS STARTED arriving the next morning—a dozen Double Delight roses, creamy with deep red edges. Heather should have sent them back, because the next day *two* dozen roses were delivered. She was just glad that Bud was on vacation this week and wasn't aware what was going on.

The chocolates didn't come until that afternoon. The box was huge and golden, with the word *Godiva* engraved on top.

"You certainly got some guy's attention," Linda, her cubicle mate, said.

"You know what this is, don't you?" Heather said, even as she opened the box and dug in, starting with a dark chocolate truffle. "It's a perfect example of mee foo saa," she mumbled while devouring the candy.

"Mee foo saa?" Linda repeated with a frown.

"The meat-for-sex theory," Heather said, once her mouth was empty.

"I must have missed that one in my marketing classes."

"Prehistoric men would hunt and bring back the choicest pieces of meat for their women, who would reward them with sex. Modern men do the same thing with gifts like flowers or candy."

Linda shrugged. "You know how it is. Men want sex. We women want romance."

"Ah, but men use romance to get sex," Heather stated, holding out the box of chocolates to Linda.

Linda gave her a dubious and humorous look as she accepted the offer of a candy. "You're saying they use romance...and meat?"

"What are you two talking about?" Nita demanded as she walked in and leaned against the wall of the cubicle.

"Heather's meat-for-sex theory," Linda replied.

"Doesn't work," Nita stated. "I've tried it."

"IT'S THURSDAY AFTERNOON and you're listening to *Love on the Rocks.* Today we've been talking about the thrill of the chase. I'm telling you, this issue dates back to Greek mythology, when the god Apollo pursued a cute nymph named Daphne. The more she ran, the more he wanted her." Heather tapped her finger against the mythology book she had spread out on the table in front of the console. "So give us a call and tell us your tale of pursuit. The number is 555-Love. Go ahead, Tina from Tinley Park."

"You were just talking about dating Greeks. Well, I dated a Greek guy once and—"

"I said the thrill of the chase dated back to Greek mythology. I wasn't talking about dating Greeks."

"Oh, then you don't want to hear about my date with Spyros?"

"Did he chase you?"

"You bet. And he was wearing one of those sexy string bikinis at the time. He's an exotic dancer. Anyway, he caught me the third time around the dining room table.''

"And thus the Olympics were born," Heather said, grinning. "Next we have Curt from Cal City."

"This pursuit thing has to do with hunting and deer. You know, like when you see a deer in the woods you want to shoot it."

"Well, actually, Curt, when I see Bambi, shooting the little creature is *not* the first thought that comes to mind."

"That's because you're a woman. Men are hunters. And if you run, then you're fair game."

"Thanks for that intellectual perspective," Heather said. "I guess that explains why men chase each other in so many sports. Anything that runs, except panty hose, is fair game."

THE CHASE CONTINUED that very night at a charity dinner dance for the American Cancer Society. Heather wasn't expecting to see Jason there. He didn't look surprised to see her, however.

"Nita, you traitor," Heather muttered as they sat down at a large banquet table marked WMAX radio. "Did you tell Jason the station had a table reserved for this event tonight?"

"*Moi?* Would I do a thing like that?"

"You bet your booties you would."

"My booties seem to have caught the attention of our waiter," Nita said, rearranging the wickedly low plunging neckline on her black evening dress as she ordered a martini for herself.

"Forget the waiter. What about Jason?"

"I talk to so many people in the course of a day, I can't recall if I said something to him or not." When Heather growled and picked up her salad fork, Nita relented. "Okay, okay, I did tell him. He made me."

"He held a gun to your head?"

"He called me and charmed it out of me."

"Yeah, he's real good at that," Heather muttered.

"You don't have anything to worry about. You're dressed to kill tonight. That's a dynamite gown."

"I didn't even remember I had it until I found it in my closet. The tags were still on it." The dark plum color made her skin look like cream. At least that's what the cabbie had told her. And there was plenty of skin showing. The dress was a classic study in seduction, the kind of gown that whispered, "Come closer, I have something to tell you." It made her feel beautiful even if she wasn't.

"Jason came stag tonight, just in case you were wondering," Nita teased.

"I wasn't wondering," Heather snapped.

"Liar!"

"Listen, this isn't my radio show you're trying to produce here, this is my life," Heather hissed.

"Who couldn't use a little help with their life?"

"Me."

"Right. You've got everything under control." Nita made a face.

"No. Control is Jason's thing, not mine," Heather said defensively.

"Jason's thing looks very good in that tuxedo. Do you mind if I go check him out a little closer?"

"Of course not," Heather said, lying. "Go right ahead."

"I would, but you're gripping my arm in a vise. I think you've cut off my circulation," Nita said dryly.

"I'm just trying to prevent you from making a fool of yourself."

"Ladies." The sound of Jason's voice made Heather's backbone stiffen and her hand fell to her lap. "This is a pleasant surprise."

"It's a surprise, all right," Heather muttered with a dark look in Nita's direction. Plastering on her best PR smile, she turned to face Jason.

Thankfully, he was wearing his glasses. He was made for formal clothes; they went well with his formal attitude. Then she remembered him wearing a black T-shirt and jeans, seducing her with his mouth and hands on her couch.

"Forget it!"

Her self-directed words were overheard by Jason. "Forget what?"

"Whatever it was you had in mind."

"I had dancing in mind. After dinner. With you, the most beautiful woman here."

His smooth compliment did not impress her because she knew it was an outrageous lie. How dare he call her beautiful! Did he think she was stupid? She looked good but not beautiful. "You don't know what you're talking about."

"On the contrary, I know exactly what I'm talking about." Taking her hand in his, he brushed his lips against her fingers.

Where had he learned how to do that? she wondered, before belatedly snatching her traitorous fingers back. How dare they tremble, letting him know he got to her? And he did know. She could see the triumphant look in his dark eyes.

Little did he know that when the occasion warranted it, she could be a damn good ice princess. And tonight, the occasion warranted it.

So after a dinner she only picked at, she was ready when Jason came to claim his dance with her. Though she accepted, she borrowed from the best, Katharine Hepburn in *Philadelphia Story.* She kept her chin and her eyes raised while wrapping herself in an invisible cloak of haughty elegance and pride.

Being invisible, that cloak didn't prevent Jason from running his fingers down her bare back to the place where her gown began. Why hadn't she noticed how low the back was on this dress?

"For someone who loves to talk, you certainly are quiet tonight," Jason noted, repeating his stealthy caress with seductive intent.

She stepped on his foot, accidentally on purpose. "I'm sorry," she said sweetly. "I'm not a very good dancer."

He smiled down at her, dimple flashing. "You're fast enough in a pair of in-line skates."

"So were you," she retorted, remembering that kiss they'd shared on the park bench. She tried to take a step away from his tempting body, but he refused to let her go. This wasn't dancing, it was embracing to music. And he was doing it on purpose, darn him.

"I don't recall you complaining at the time."

He was watching her, the gleam in his eye nearly

impossible to resist while the huskiness of his voice was equally devastating to her defenses. She had to turn her face away from his perceptive gaze to stare over his shoulder or else risk melting all over him. "Well, I'm complaining now," she declared. "You're holding me so tightly I can't breathe."

He loosened his hold ever so slightly. "Better?"

Better would be on the other side of the room, where he couldn't practice his seductive art on her. And he was most definitely a pro at this. He danced as well as he played the sax, smoothly but with darker undertones that drew you in and captured you before you knew it.

She had to say something, anything to get her mind off the sweet magic singing through her body as a result of being held so closely against his body. "What does your coffee mug look like?"

Her abrupt question clearly threw him. "What?"

"You heard me." Her confidence was returning. "Your coffee mug. What's written on it?"

"Nothing," he replied. "It's black and it doesn't have anything written on it."

"I knew it."

"Why am I getting the impression that I just failed some kind of test here?" He'd never witnessed a regal shrug before. She had the movement down pat. "Come on, talk to me," he coaxed her. "What does your coffee mug have written on it?"

"No Trespassing."

He tried not to grin. "See? That was easy enough. Now how about something a little more challenging? How about telling me your hopes and fears?"

"Syndication and tornadoes."

Jason couldn't take his eyes off her. He'd never seen her so distant and desirable. Although she'd swept her hair up, plenty of strands still tumbled down around her face, giving her a look that made him long to run his fingers through the colorful silkiness.

"Your hair looks different tonight. There's more gold in it."

"Shampoo-in color," she said, hoping her prosaic answer would make him think twice about complimenting her again. A woman could only take so much. Especially a woman crazy in love—crazy being the operative word.

Bending down, he nuzzled her ear, his tongue actually darting out to circle her dainty diamond stud earring.

"Stop that!"

"You've still got your Balance," he murmured appreciatively.

Where did he get an idea like that? It felt like she had two left feet and a pair of rubbery knees.

"Your perfume," he elaborated with a knowing grin. "Balance, you said."

"Am I supposed to be impressed that you remembered?"

"Impressed would be nice," he agreed, loosening his hold on her slightly, but remaining close enough that his thighs continued to brush against her with every sway to the music. His hand traveled up her bare back again. "Responsive and melting is even better."

"Don't hold your breath." Her words would have sounded more forceful had her voice not been trembling.

"You've already taken my breath away. I don't have any left."

Heather didn't have much resistance left, but it was just enough to see her back to her chair after the music stopped. A second longer and she'd have been a goner. As it was she'd left his arms with a mixture of reluctance and relief that did not bode well for her future peace of mind.

JASON WAS UP TO his elbows in paperwork when Anastasia stopped by his loft Friday night. She always entered a room like a tornado and tonight was no exception. "You told me that if I dropped these nonprofit organization forms off, you'd look them over for me." Her golden eyes gleamed at him hopefully.

"What lost cause have you taken up this time?"

"Historic preservation and it's not a lost cause. Speaking of lost causes—" she lowered her voice to a whisper while glancing around the living room "—where's Dad?"

"He had tickets for the Cubs game tonight. And you should show more respect for your father."

"He should show more common sense," she retorted in exasperation. "Mom is really mad at him this time."

"For what?" Jason ran his hands through his hair, which was only slightly darker than his sister's. "Because he grunts? The man has been grunting forever."

"Dad told you this was about his grunting? He's

denser than I thought and so are you for believing him.''

"Then what is this about?''

"Communication. Appreciation. The only time he talks to mom is when he's complaining about how she does the wash or cooks dinner. Now that he's home all the time, she thought they'd be able to do things together, but he just sits in front of the TV like a couch potato. She's told him how she feels but he doesn't listen. Like someone else I know.'' His sister gave Jason an impatient glare. "You said you were going to talk to him.''

Jason tried not to feel guilty. "I meant to, but time got away from me.''

"And now you've got Dad living with you.''

"Not living,'' he hurriedly corrected her, "just staying. Temporarily.''

"You hope. When are you going to get some furniture in here?'' she demanded, plopping down on the S-shaped leather couch that looked better than it felt. "Doesn't all this chrome and stainless steel give you the chills?''

"I hired a top designer to do this place.''

Anastasia was not impressed. "It lacks heart.''

Jason thought about Heather's house, cluttered with pieces that each had personal meaning to her. Compared to her home, the loft was a little on the sterile side. But he didn't like feeling crowded. Not after having his siblings living in his back pockets growing up. He needed lots of elbow room, both physically and emotionally.

But he wasn't getting that with his dad staying with

him. Whenever he tried to broach the topic of his returning home, his dad changed the subject. Jason didn't know what to do, so he did nothing, hoping things would work themselves out and that his dad would get tired of sleeping in the guest room. So far that hadn't happened. Jason planned on giving it until Sunday before taking matters into his own hands.

"What are you doing home on a Friday night?" Anastasia asked.

Jason had been asking himself that same question. He'd tried calling Heather and had only gotten her answering machine at home and her voice mail at work for the past two days.

"I've got work to do," Jason answered.

"What are you working on?" Anastasia asked, picking up the yellow legal pad he'd left on the couch.

"Give that back to me."

Anastasia leaped out of his reach, just as she had when they were kids.

"I don't believe this!" she exclaimed after reading his precise writing. "You've actually made a step-by-step plan to seduce poor Heather. You've even made a list of pros and cons!"

She didn't have to tell him that; he already had the list memorized.

"What's this about a dessert-cart incident?" Anastasia asked.

"Give that back to me!" he growled.

His sister was one of the few women on the face of the planet unimpressed by his glowering expression. "Hey, I know you're an obsessive list maker, but I can't believe you've actually made up a list like this.''

"That's the logical thing to do, not that you'd know anything about that, flying by the emotional seat of your pants as you always do.''

"I see you've already crossed off step one, talking to her face-to-face. And step two, send flowers and chocolate. That's real original, bro.''

"Did it ever occur to you that being original isn't all it's cracked up to be?''

"No. I like original.''

"That's obvious." His sister was dressed in one of her infamous thrift-shop outfits of a man's tailored shirt tied in a knot over a skirt that went down to her ankles. A pair of combat boots completed the picture, which wasn't a pretty one in his estimation. But then his sister never listened to him. "I don't like original.''

"What about Heather? She's the one you're trying to please.''

That gave him pause for a moment. "She likes original," he grudgingly admitted. "But she likes flowers and chocolate, too.''

"You know this for a fact?''

"What woman doesn't like flowers and chocolate? Besides, her friend told me exactly what kind she likes.''

"Jason, Jason." Anastasia shook her head in sisterly indulgence. "Anyone can send her flowers or candy. You've got a thing or two to learn about women.''

"I seem to have done pretty damn well by myself all these years."

"You've had women chase you, but this one doesn't seem to follow that pattern, bless her heart. I think I like her already."

"You'd like anyone and anything that gives me trouble," Jason grumbled.

Anastasia grinned. "You've got that right. Who is this Heather woman? Does she have a last name?"

Jason wasn't about to tell her Heather was that *Love on the Rocks* woman who had incited their mother to send their father packing. He didn't trust Anastasia not to side with Heather and their mom. "Isn't it time for you to leave now?"

"I'm going. But before I do, let me give you this piece of advice. Women like a man with imagination. A man with some soul. I know you've got some hidden deep down inside you someplace because I've heard you jamming at the club. Tap into that, Jase. Unless you want to get lost in the crowd of stuffed shirts."

"I hate being called Jase."

"I know." She tossed his legal pad at him. "That's why I do it. Call me about those nonprofit papers when you're through looking at them."

"Don't hold your breath," Jason called after her, even though he knew he'd get back to her in a few days. But first he had a woman to seduce. Heather.

"YOU CAN STOP SQUINTING. She's not out in the audience, man," Natron told him Sunday night, after Jason sat in on the early set.

"I left a message on her machine inviting her to the club tonight."

"Wise move. Last time you played for her, she was offering to have sex with you."

Natron was a good friend, but Jason couldn't confess what Heather's *real* reason for being at the club that night had been. It only served to prove what an idiot he was, and the fewer people who knew that the better. Meanwhile, he had to come up with a way of snagging Heather the way she'd tried to snag him. He murmured his thoughts aloud. "Maybe I should play for her again."

"Maybe you should. You know what they say, man. If Mahomet won't come to the mountain, then the mountain has to go to Mahomet."

AFTER GETTING ONLY four hours of sleep for two nights in a row because of brooding about Jason, Heather had gone to bed by ten. She was exhausted.

She closed her eyes, only to dream yet again about Jason. She could even hear him playing his sax while she played him, running her fingers over his body, as his music got louder and louder, stronger and stronger.

She blinked, disoriented and surprised to find herself awake. But the music continued. A quick glance at her bedside table told her that it was nearly two in the morning.

Was her neighbor, the stockbroker, having a party or something? No, the sound was coming from directly beneath her bedroom window, from her terrace. And it was definitely a saxophone.

Grabbing a robe to cover her cotton nightie, she tiptoed to the window to peek between the slats of her venetian blinds. It was pitch black outside but she did see the flash of light on metal. Looking closer, she saw the saxophone. She still couldn't see the man playing it.

She could have turned on the terrace lights, but for some reason she didn't want to do that. Too much light might make the dreamlike scene disappear.

Then the music suddenly stopped. Instead she heard the sound of pebbles hitting her bedroom window.

She opened the window. There was only one man it could be. "Jason?" Her voice was soft.

His wasn't. It was as loud and clear as all get out. "No. It's the Dark Knight."

"What are you doing?"

"Getting your attention."

"It's two in the morning!" Mr. Jones her elderly neighbor bellowed. "Shut up out there or I'll call the cops!"

"Ask for Detective Abromski," Jason shouted back. "He's a friend of mine."

Heather couldn't believe it. Her stuffy, uptight prosecutor was actually on her terrace in the middle of the night. Well, actually his alter ego, the Dark Knight, was on her terrace, serenading her with his sexy sax. He was dressed in black jeans and T-shirt, radiating the dauntless audacity of a knight.

The question was, should she let down the moat bridge and let him in?

9

"RAPUNZEL, RAPUNZEL, let down your sweet hair," Jason shouted up to her.

"I'm calling the cops on the count of three," Mr. Jones yelled. "One…"

"Don't do that, I'm letting him in now," Heather shouted back. To Jason, she said, "Stay there, I'll be down in a minute to let you in the terrace sliding door. And don't make any more noise."

That last request was made in vain as she heard the crash of him apparently bumping into one of her many potted plants.

Heather and her cat both met Jason at the terrace door. Jason greeted the cat first. "Maxie, old boy, old friend!" Jason set down his battered, black musical-instrument case to pet Maxie behind the ears just as he liked. "How's it going?"

"Are you drunk?" Heather asked suspiciously.

"Only with the vision of you," Jason replied, his eyes gleaming in the semidarkness. He wasn't wearing his glasses. "I trust those weren't man-eating Venus's-flytraps out on your terrace?"

"You trust correctly." The problem was that Heather couldn't trust. Couldn't trust that he wouldn't break her heart. But she also couldn't keep fighting something she wanted so badly. Having been apart from Jason made her miss him more than she thought humanly possible.

Looking at him, she whispered, "I really thought I could get over you."

"I thought the same thing about you. I was wrong."

"So was I."

A second later, she was in his arms. His lips claimed hers with such commanding persuasion that she was soon lost in the intimacies of his tongue moving against hers. He bound her to him with butterfly-soft caresses and arms wrapped around her so tightly that she never wanted him to let her go. Unless it was to lead him to her bedroom. Because this time she wanted to do this right.

Murmuring her intentions between nibbling kisses, she tugged the hem of his dark T-shirt from the waistband of his black jeans. Jason contributed to the effort by kicking off first one shoe and then the other as he moved with her across the living room toward the stairs leading up to her bedroom.

They left a trail of clothing behind, most of it his, as she wasn't wearing much. They didn't actually get his T-shirt off until the third step. It was left there, along with her robe.

By the time they reached her bedroom, Jason was barefoot and bare chested. The top snap on his black jeans was undone and his hair was tousled, falling over his forehead just the way she liked it.

She could hardly believe he was here, in her bedroom. His dark masculinity was a stark contrast to the light femininity of their surroundings. The walls and drapes were white, the main sense of color coming from the pale pink, cutwork duvet cover on her bed. The double-wedding-ring quilt with its pastel rings on a white background looked great on the wall above the bed, but Heather nearly knocked it onto the floor as Jason tumbled her onto her bed.

"I haven't forgotten that you like going slow." His grin was contagious. "Now that I've got you where I want you, I'll go *real* slow," he promised her, his voice husky, his gaze possessive.

Heather didn't know what to say so she blurted out, "Did you bring any protection?" and then felt like yanking the covers over her head. She'd offered her listeners a million funny ways to bring up the subject of safe sex, but when it came time for her to talk about it she'd sounded like an awkward, overeager novice.

Jason didn't appear to mind, though. Instead, he slowly smiled as he retrieved several latex condoms from his wallet.

"Did you know I'd let you in tonight?"

"All I knew was that I couldn't go another night without seeing you."

His words melted her nervousness away. "Come here," she whispered, holding her arms out to him. As he stood before her, she finished the task of undoing his zipper. The stretchy material of his white Jockey shorts strained against his surging desire. Her knuckles gently brushed against him as she lowered his jeans down around his hips.

Growling her name, Jason kicked off his jeans and

tumbled her back on the bed, his hot body conforming to hers with an exquisite fit. He ran his hands over her, eliminating her nightgown with one economic move. She could feel the rubbing of his bare thighs against hers as she explored his body with wondering fingertips.

He was such an enigma. A man who loved control, yet had the power to destroy it in her. A man with an aura of calmness and concentration who had the ability to make her soul sing with his music or his smile. The creator of the best and only eye sex she'd ever had. The man she loved.

His obvious desire for her gave her the confidence she'd lacked. Beauty could indeed be a state of mind, not of body. Which meant she was no longer panicked about him seeing her naked. There was no time for panic, no room for it as she was consumed with need.

His ragged breathing was audible as she skimmed her hands over his back with slow precision, as if mapping every male inch and needing to record it for posterity. He rewarded her scouting expedition with a series of heated kisses from her temple to the corner of her mouth.

Closing her eyes to further enjoy the temptations of his lips, she now had to rely completely on her sense of touch to give her a picture of him. The provocative pressure of his muscled body provided her with ample material. She had no idea how much time passed before her fingers reached the elastic waistband of his briefs. There she paused to swirl her nails against the small of his back.

He repaid her by spreading kisses from her jaw to

her throat to the top of her breast. There he swirled his tongue in a lazy figure eight that drove her crazy with anticipation.

"If you want to do this slowly," he whispered, his voice as raspy as sandpaper, "then we've got to—"

"Do this?" she whispered back, her smile sultry as she removed his underwear, tossing it over her shoulder.

"Then I suppose you'd like it if I did this." Jason dispatched her silky panties with equal flair.

"I'd like it even better if you did this," she murmured, taking his hand and guiding it to her.

She was vocal in her pleasure, her increasing pants turning into moans and breathless gasps. Then she shattered in his arms.

When her eyelids fluttered open, she gazed at him with dazed appreciation. And a look of feminine anticipation. "Now you," she murmured, her voice running over him like hot satin, just as her fingers and lips trailed over him, bringing him dangerously close to peaking.

His fingers trembled as he took care of protection, before returning to the cradle of her body. She welcomed him. His entry was smooth and swift, as was his sigh of bliss. With iron control, he kept the rhythm easy, his movements filling her with joy as he prolonged their ultimate satisfaction as long as he could.

Keeping his eyes on her, he saw the heated flush of passion on her cheeks, tasted the swollen lushness of her mouth as she resumed those breathless pants that drove him wild.

And still he rocked against her, letting her take all

of him as he buried himself in her deepest recesses, until his control finally shattered, as hers had. Shouting her name, he arched his back. Surging into her, he climaxed as never before.

WHEN THE ALARM went off the next morning, Heather was alone in her bed. Had it all been a dream? Had she only imagined that Jason had made love like no one had ever made love to her before?

No, she could still feel the warmth on the sheets left from his body, still smell him on her pillowcase. Hugging the pillow, she stretched languidly.

So much for her plans to stay away from Jason. It had been impossible. She couldn't even find it in her heart to feel any regret, except for the fact that he hadn't been here when she'd woken up.

Why had he left? Had *he* felt regret? Had he noticed how big her thighs were? Had he leaped out of her bed as if he couldn't wait to get away? Had she slept with her mouth hanging open?

Something crinkled as she shifted uneasily. Tugging the pillow away from her face, she saw the note he'd left for her.

Jason's handwriting was as contradictory as he was—controlled strokes with bold flourishes. She ran her fingers over the words. He'd had an early court appearance and hadn't wanted to wake her. He'd be in touch.

She frowned at that last sentence. It sounded pretty vague. But then she read on. He'd written one word and underlined it twice: *Soon!*

JASON WASN'T EXACTLY SURE what he expected to accomplish by coming to see Heather at the radio station during his lunch break on Monday. He wasn't exactly sure about a lot of things.

It had seemed so simple when he'd set out on this plan for revenge. His desire to teach her a lesson had gelled with his desire to get her into bed. His strategy had worked. She'd ended up naked in his arms. But having sex with her hadn't decreased his need for her. It had only strengthened it. Which made him very uneasy.

He hadn't tossed the bet in her face this morning. While still furious about the way she'd used him, Jason's innate sense of honor cringed from hurting her that way. Instead, while she slept, he'd hurriedly gotten dressed and hightailed it out of there after scribbling her a brief note.

Some revenge-taker he was. When it came down to the crunch he froze. Getting even with her wasn't supposed to affect him this deeply.

He was supposed to spend the night and then toss her aside. Not that he had any experience treating women that way. Maybe that was his problem. He was too nice a guy.

Making love with Heather hadn't gotten her out of his system. It had only intensified his fascination with her. She continued to rattle him. He honestly didn't know where they'd go from here. He only knew he had to see her again.

Acting on a whim, he stopped en route and picked up a bunch of balloons and a single Double Delight rose at the florist shop in the foyer. Was he still seducing her for revenge, or had it turned into the real thing? Jason couldn't be sure and he refused to examine his motives too closely, because doing so only turned his stomach into knots and struck fear in his heart, neither of which were conditions that appealed to him.

Jason checked his watch as WMAX's dedicated elevator whisked him directly to the seventh floor and the radio station's operations. His timing was good—Heather's show wouldn't be starting for another ninety minutes yet.

When he gave his name and asked to see Heather, the receptionist took one look at the balloons and flashed him a knowing grin before waving him on by, her directions unintelligible due to the gum she was chomping.

As he followed what looked to be a main hallway, Jason took note of the poster-size PR photos of the various radio personalities that hung along the walls. Jason thought Heather was much better looking in person than her PR photo, which was a shadowy version of herself.

"Excuse me." He stopped a heavy-set man wearing a yellow jacket and pea green tie. For some reason he looked vaguely familiar, but Jason couldn't place him. "Can you tell me where I can find Heather Grayson?"

The stubby man waved a cigar at him. "Who wants to know?"

"I'm Jason Knight."

"WE HAVE TO FIND JASON before Bud says something to him!" Heather yanked open the door leading from the break room out to the hallway. The moment Nita had come to tell her that Jason had been spotted in the hallway, blind panic had taken hold, hence the cherry yogurt stain on her favorite purple sweater. Heather's matching floral skirt swirled around her legs as she came to an abrupt stop. "Where did Linda say she saw him when she called you?"

"At the reception desk."

Frantically looking both ways, she saw no sign of Jason. "You go that way," she told Nita, pointing ahead of them toward the reception area. "I'll keep looking back here."

Running to the intersection of two corridors, she immediately noticed a huge bunch of shiny Mylar balloons at one end. She thought a deliveryman was holding them, but then she caught sight of the well-cut dark suit. That was no deliveryman, that was Jason. He was almost completely blocked from her view by...Bud.

Oh no, oh no, oh no, oh no. She was hyperventilating. *Stay calm, stay calm, stay calm.* Maybe it would be all right. Maybe Bud wouldn't say anything about the bet. Maybe he hadn't had time to.

Maybe, maybe, please, please.

She joined them as quickly as she could without running.

"Ah, there you are, Heather." Bud's malicious smile made her stomach drop. "I was just telling Jason here how I was responsible for the two of you meeting in the first place."

Heather had to get rid of Bud pronto. She knew of

only one way to do that. "Bud, there's an urgent phone call for you. It's…Michael Jordan—you know, M.J.—and he wants to talk to you immediately. Some kind of exclusive interview thing. You'd better go."

Bud looked at her as if he couldn't be sure if she was lying or not. She knew that the chance of an exclusive one-on-one with Chicago's biggest sports figure was too tempting to resist.

"You don't want to keep M.J. waiting, Bud."

"Right. Well, Jason, good luck. Not that you'll need it. Not with Heather here."

She cut him off. "Balloons?" Her nervous words were directed to Jason. "For me? That's great. Why don't we get out of this hallway and go somewhere more private." It wasn't a question, it was a plea. She was desperate to get away from Bud.

As she tried to drag Jason away, Bud got in his final salvo.

"Yeah, Heather, you snagged him all right," he said. "Just like you said you would."

10

HEATHER FROZE. Snagged! He'd said snagged. In front of Jason.

"Well, I guess I'll leave you two lovebirds alone to talk," Bud cheerfully declared, clearly satisfied now that he'd done his dirty deed for the day.

Maybe Jason hadn't heard. Maybe he hadn't understood the reference.

He had. One look at his face told her that much. But the look in his eyes told her he wasn't surprised.

"You knew," she whispered in disbelief. "You already knew."

"About the bet? Yes, I knew."

How could he sound so calm? "How did you find out? Why didn't you say anything?"

Bud's smirking face had rekindled Jason's anger about being the butt of their prank. As a result, his voice was hard and curt. "Because I wanted to teach you a lesson."

"When did you find out?"

"A while ago. I overheard you and Nita talking." Jason went on to name the restaurant.

Heather scrambled to put the pieces together as she reconstructed the past few days in her head. She and Nita had eaten there after she'd told Jason she didn't

want to see him anymore. Which meant that he'd
known about the bet when he started chasing her.

It was beginning to make sense. And it was beginning to make Heather furious. "You said you wanted
to teach me a lesson. What kind of lesson? That
you're as bad as I am?"

"Hey, I'm the injured party here!" Jason retorted,
irritation flashing in his dark eyes. "You're the one
who started this with your little bet between you and
your co-workers."

"That was before I knew you. What's your excuse?"

"I don't like being lied to or made a fool of."

"I never tried to make a fool out of you," Heather
said in a rush. "The whole thing started out...it was
just a bet."

"Just a bet?" he roared.

She wasn't saying any of this right. "I did what I
did because Bud challenged my professional credentials regarding relationships. He held up that magazine with you on the cover and made this outrageous
wager. I didn't really take him seriously, but the next
thing I knew everyone in the office started placing
their bets—"

Anger was now foremost in his gaze as he cut her
off. "So that's why the receptionist gave me that
strange grin. She'd placed her bet on you. And when
I showed up with a bunch of balloons and flowers
like a lovesick puppy, she knew she'd won."

"I didn't ask you to bring me balloons or flowers.
That was *your* idea. Part of *your* master plan. You've

heard my reasons for doing what I did, how about yours?''

"I told you, I don't like being made a fool of. Do you know that my mother has tossed my father out and he's living with me thanks to you?''

Heather blinked at this non sequitur. "What are you talking about?''

"Thanks to your stupid talk show my father is sleeping in my guest room, losing my TV's remote and playing his damn Dean Martin record over and over again until I think I'm going to go crazy.''

"You *are* crazy.''

"If I am, you made me that way,'' he shot back angrily. "Starting with that damn bet of yours.''

"At least I called it off before you and I...before we...''

"Had sex?'' Jason curtly interjected.

His words shot a hole in her heart.

"Exactly. The same can't be said for you. What was your little plan? To get your revenge by seducing me and making me think you cared about me? By making me care about you?''

He didn't bother denying it. "Did you care?''

Heather wasn't about to humiliate herself any further by confessing her feelings for him. She didn't dare open her mouth, afraid of the words that might spill out, so she shook her head.

Jason's face darkened. "It wasn't me you were interested in. It was Chicago's Sexiest Bachelor. It didn't matter who the poor sap was. Your job was to snag him.'' Anger compressed his lips into a grim line as he growled, "I don't need that kind of dishonesty in my life. I'm out of here.'' He shoved the balloons at her. "You might as well keep these, they're as full of hot air as you are!"

Tears clogged her throat as she helplessly watched him storm off.

Damn. Damn. Damn! She wished more than ever that she'd never agreed to the stupid bet. She may have nearly won the wager, but she had definitely lost Jason.

"REALLY, BETTY, I can't believe how badly you've botched this assignment." Hattie anxiously fiddled with the sunflowers in her straw hat as she perched atop a picture frame in the radio station hallway.

"Like you could do any better, Miss Smartypants," Betty retorted from her perch on the next frame down the hall.

"I can. And I will when we deal with Anastasia. I'm so glad I got the girl baby." Hattie added with a satisfied pat to her silvery curls.

"She's not a baby anymore, and she's not going to be any easier than Jason," Muriel said, tugging a bag of granola out of one of her many vest pockets. "Now Ryan is another story. There's a man I can easily deal with. Finding his soul mate is next on our assignment roster."

"We're getting way ahead of ourselves here, girls. First we've got to close the case on Jason," Betty reminded her sisters.

"And it's not looking good at the moment," Hattie said.

"That's an understatement." Exasperated, Betty shoved her bangs off her forehead.

"What happens if Jason and his soul mate don't get together?" Hattie's voice was uncertain.

Betty shuddered. "Trust me, you don't want to know."

Hattie sighed. "I hate to see them both so upset."

"What about us?" Muriel retorted. "They've certainly upped my stress level. And I hate to think what my blood pressure must be."

"I thought one of the advantages of being a fairy godmother was not having to worry about things like blood pressure." Hattie's nervous fingers had reduced the sunflowers on her hat to little pieces.

"I've just about had it with those two lunkheads," Betty muttered. "I'm ready to do something drastic…"

"Wait!" Hattie zoomed over to grab Betty's hand before she tugged her left ear and initiated whatever drastic measure she'd been about to take. The picture frame Hattie had been perched on swung drunkenly on the wall as a result of her abrupt departure. "Jason and Heather saw the light on their own once before. Maybe they'll do it again."

"That's a real big maybe," Muriel inserted. "You do realize that if we mess up, we won't be getting any more chances."

Muriel and Hattie both looked worried. For once, Betty's expression matched theirs.

"WHAT EXACTLY DO WE need men for? That's the topic this afternoon on *Love on the Rocks*." Heather tugged up the long sleeves on her purple sweater before readjusting her headphones and moving closer to the mike. "Give us a call with your views. Go ahead Bonnie from Buffalo Grove, you're on the air."

"How about rodent control?"

"What about it? When you say rodent, are you referring to mice or men?"

"I meant that men can be good for rodent control. You know, catching mice and stuff."

"My cat is better at it than most men are. I should show you the e-mail I got from my friend Judy in New York City. Suffice it to say that when she needed a mouse catcher, the only male of any use was an eight-year-old bed wetter, and he demanded to be paid for his work." Heather added the gong sound effect before saying, "Thanks for calling, Bonnie. Next we have Fran from Franklin Park."

"Hi, Heather, I listen to your show all the time and I'm a big fan. Anyway, I was wondering why men have such trouble having a normal conversation with a woman. Especially on the weekends. My husband turns on the cable sports channel and that's it. There's no communicating with him. The weekend is the only time for fixing up our house, or doing errands and stuff. My daughter's room needs painting and he promised he'd do it. That was back before Christmas. It's nearly the end of May now. When I ask him, he just mumbles, 'Yeah, I'll get to it.'"

"Sounds like M.A.S. to me. Male answering syndrome. Indicated by grunts of agreement, or disagreement, regardless of what you're saying."

"Is there a cure?"

"The recovery rate isn't real good but it does improve drastically when the TV is off."

"He wouldn't let me do that. When we go out to a store he even brings a little TV that hangs around his neck."

"Have you ever thought of just leaving him in the store and going home without him? Or maybe pick up a new model while you're out shopping. Good luck, Fran. Next we have Al from Arlington Heights."

"Hey, I think you're being a little hard on men today. You make us sound much worse than we are."

"Pretty difficult to do."

"Yeah, well, my wife and I have been married twenty-five years. We just had a huge fight. I got a letter from the IRS because my wife didn't fill out the forms correctly. I didn't want her to do the taxes herself, but she insisted, and I gave in to her demands and this is what happens. Everything is a mess and it was all her fault."

His words hit Heather the wrong way as she took up the cause of yet another woman accused by a thick-skulled man. Her fury abruptly boiled over. "I see. So just because she made one little mistake on your income tax, you're going to toss years of marriage out the window. That's just great, Al!" She ignored the frantic cut-it-out motions Nita was making on the other side of the booth window. Heather was just getting going. She wasn't about to calm down now. "You know what should go out the window? Sanctimonious guys like you!" She disconnected the call.

Are you nuts? Nita typed on Heather's screen. *He just wanted to know whether to bring her flowers or candy after their fight.*

"And to answer Al's unspoken question about whether to bring his poor wife flowers or candy, he should bring himself home first. Flowers and candy are optional. All she needs is him begging her forgiveness, him back in her arms again. Now let's hear a word from Rosie's Florist."

"Great," Nita said as she joined Heather in the broadcast booth during the commercial break. "First you insult a caller, then you tell your listening audience that flowers are optional right before we air a florist's ad. Nice going."

"You told me to fight back."

"I didn't mean to fight our advertisers! Or our audience. Take it easy, okay? We're back in fifteen seconds."

But Heather wasn't about to pull any punches now. She leaned into the mike, her voice confidential and rich with feminine outrage. "You know, you might have heard the saying that men want sex and women want romance. What women really want is a *relationship*. Men use romance to get sex. They serenade you beneath your bedroom window, then they dump you. If you've ever been dumped, give us a call."

That certainly got listeners' attention. The phone lines lit up like Michigan Avenue at Christmastime.

"Talk to me, Grace from Gurnee."

"My boyfriend dumped me last year. He said that I talked too much. And then I just read in some book that men don't want women to talk in complete sentence while having sex. Is that true?''

"There are men who don't want women to talk in complete sentences at *any* time. Let me guess, that book was written by a man, right?''

"Yes.''

"I knew it. I say we shoot him.'' Heather shot a look at Nita's apoplectic face in the production booth. "Hey, I was just kidding.''

Nita sagged with relief.

"Burning at the stake might be better,'' Heather decided. "We could gather around a big bonfire…hey, what's going on?'' she demanded as she heard the sudden sound of a cat litter jingle coming from the headphones covering her ears. "We weren't supposed to go to a commercial yet.''

"You've gone off the deep end. I'm playing a tape of an earlier show. It was that or watch you self-destruct on the air.''

"I thought you were the one who liked telling it like it is.''

"I do, but you're going overboard.'' Nita sounded exasperated, a rare occurrence for her. "You've got to get hold of yourself! Go home. Get some rest. Get a new perspective on things. Everything will look better tomorrow. Provided we both still have jobs,'' she tacked on darkly.

FOR A MAN WHO didn't like surprises, Jason had sure been getting more than his fair share of them lately.

The most recent came when he arrived home Monday night, switched on the light and found his father sprawled across the leather couch with a giggling woman beneath him.

"All right, that does it, Dad!" Jason's bellow startled the cozy-twosome. "I've been patient, but this is too much..."

His voice trailed off as he caught sight of the woman's face. "Mom?"

Her salt-and-pepper hair was mussed as if she'd forgotten to brush it. And her cheeks were red...was that stubble burn? What had they been up to? On second thought, he didn't want to know.

"What's going on here? I mean, it looks like you two have kissed and made up."

His mother's pretty blush confirmed it. "Your father called me this afternoon. I came over and we talked in front of the fireplace. It was romantic, like being a guest in a resort or something. One thing led to another..."

"And then you walked in." His dad didn't look very pleased about that.

"So is everything...settled?" Jason asked.

"If it is, it's thanks to Heather."

"Heather?" Jason repeated. "What are you talking about?"

"I listened to her show today," his dad admitted. "Boy, you should have heard her going after men. Someone had certainly put a bee in her bonnet today."

Jason shifted uncomfortably, knowing darn well that *he* was that someone.

"Anyway," his dad continued, "She talked about this thing called M.A.S."

"Male answering syndrome," his mom interjected.

"And it got me thinking that maybe I had a touch of that M.A.S."

"More than just a touch, dear." His mom's words were accompanied by a wry smile and a pat to his dad's cheek.

"Anyway, your mom and I—" he hugged her "—got some important things settled. I'll be heading back home tonight."

Seeing them together—presenting a united front—made Jason feel good. Like things were right in the world again. Some of them, anyway. This was how he always thought of his parents, as being part of the same whole. His mom was much shorter than his dad, but she ruled the roost...when his dad let her. Many was the time when he was growing up that they'd danced across the kitchen while supper cooked, or organized a family camp out in the backyard to count stars in the summer.

It was only then that Jason realized that by focusing on the chaos of growing up in a crowded household, he'd forgotten the fun, the laughter, and the love. It hadn't been scheduled, hadn't been programmed. And that realization, along with the memory of Heather's stricken expression at the radio station after their fight earlier, left Jason wondering if he'd made the right choices in opting for control in his life rather than love.

In the past, Jason had avoided emotional entanglements, preferring mutual interests and physical attraction in his relationships with the opposite sex. Even the expression *falling* in love indicated a loss of control. Falling meant you lost your balance, your ability to stand on your own two feet. It meant giving up, something he hadn't wanted any part of.

Now Jason couldn't help thinking that in choosing control and revenge instead of love, maybe he'd lost far more than he could ever have anticipated.

11

THE SKYLIGHT IN her foyer acted as a night-light as Heather tiptoed past a snoozing Maxie to get to the kitchen and the fridge. She'd been too upset to eat much dinner.

Maxie opened one eye at the sound of the refrigerator door opening. He knew good things for cats were stored in there—raw meat, cooked chicken, leftovers.

Sitting at the eating nook dividing her kitchen and dining room, Heather shared her chilled can of pitted black olives with Maxie while discussing Jason.

"I wish I didn't love him so damn much," she said, choking back tears.

Maxie rubbed against her calves as if to comfort her.

"But I'll get over him, right, Maxie? The sooner, the better."

She crouched down to stroke Maxie, and he licked her nose to show how much he cared. The sandpaper roughness of his tongue was a familiar comfort.

"This is just a temporary insanity, right? Some sort of hormonal spell cast on me that made me think Jason was a knight in shining black armor. He isn't. He's just a guy like any other, only worse."

Maxie's response was to start cleaning his whiskers, the rhythmic swipe of his paw accompanied by the lap of his tongue.

"Okay, so he was *better* than any other guy where sex was concerned. That doesn't give him the right to make me think he cared about me. That's what hurts…"

Her voice trailed off as she once again blinked back the tears. From her perch atop the white stool in the kitchen, she could see across the living room to the shadows of her azaleas against the moonlit blinds leading to the terrace. She still hadn't cleaned up the mess that Jason had made out there when he'd broken one of her terra-cotta pots after serenading her. She hadn't cleaned up the mess he'd made of her broken heart, either. That one was definitely going to be harder to deal with.

When the phone rang, she and Maxie both jumped a foot. Heather hated it when a call came in the middle of the night. It always made her think something was wrong. "Hello?"

"Are you asleep?" Nita asked.

"No. What are you doing up this late?"

"Watching cable TV. How about you?"

Heather started to cry.

"That bad, huh?" Nita's voice was sympathetic.

"I screwed up big-time."

"I didn't really mean that crack about us not having jobs by tomorrow," Nita reassured her.

"I'm not talking about my job," Heather wailed. "That's what got me into trouble in the first place. Accepting that damn bet to prove I'm good at my job.

I don't know what made me do it, it's like some strange force took over and I was an observer in my own life. I'm not making excuses, I'm an adult and I take responsibility for my own actions, stupid as they may be. I'm smart enough to know that romance and bets don't mix. I should have told Jason the truth from the very beginning, maybe then we would have had a chance and none of this mess would have happened. If only I'd just been honest."

"So what are you going to do now? Give up?"

"I'm not sure," Heather said unsteadily. "Despite all my training, I still don't know what to do next. Maybe what I need is a sign from above or something. Or maybe I just need to decide what I want," she added in the next breath. "And if I want Jason, then I need to be prepared to fight for him."

WHEN HEATHER SHOWED UP for work the next day, she was a calmer, saner woman than the one who had left the day before. She was also a determined woman. She knew what she was going to do. What had to be done. She'd reached a decision during the night. At precisely 3:33 a.m., to be exact.

That's when something Jason had said during their fight finally clicked: "It wasn't *me* you were interested in." If he'd thought she was faking her interest in him, faking her feelings for him, then maybe she could straighten things out between them.

His intentions had to have been more than just to have sex with her. Why else had he come to see her at work with a handful of balloons? His plans must have gone as wildly astray as hers had, and he must feel something for her, something that had grown despite the bet, despite his desire to turn the tables on her.

She certainly hadn't planned on falling in love with Jason. And she had fallen not for Chicago's Sexiest Bachelor, but for *him*. With the way his mind worked, with the sweet music he loved to play, with the way he could look at her and make her feel beautiful.

The big unknown here was Jason's feelings for her. How often had she chided callers for not telling their partners how they felt, for expecting them to somehow instinctively know they were loved?

The bottom line was nothing ventured, nothing gained. And today she aimed on venturing plenty, the entire enchilada.

She'd dressed appropriately for this all-or-nothing battle, choosing one of her power outfits, a burgundy pantsuit with a black, sleeveless blouse that had a weskit bottom, giving her a slightly military appearance.

Which was appropriate. Because she'd made her battle plan. Now all that was left was to execute it. She planned on making her assertive move today on her show, providing she still had a show.

The first person she ran into was Bud. Surprisingly, he eyed her not with his usual disdain but with a new grudging sense of respect.

"I want to apologize for yesterday. I shouldn't have said what I did," he replied, to her utter amazement. "I guess I went too far. To make amends I called in a few markers and got some major Chicago sports figures to agree to do some of those public service spots you're organizing for that battered-women's shelter.''

"For Safe House? Oh, Bud, that's great!"

He gave her a grumpy look and took a step back, as if afraid she might hug him or something. "Yeah, well, this doesn't mean I like you or your show. I still think it's wimpy girl stuff. And I don't want you thinking I've gotten sentimental in my old age because I haven't. Just remember that.'' With those words, he took off down the hall, his smoking cigar held behind him.

Nita was waiting for Heather at her desk.

"You're not going to believe this," Heather said. "Bud actually arranged to help us out with the Safe House campaign."

"Yeah, well, you're not going to believe this. I talked to management and told them you weren't yourself yesterday. But here's the kicker. They weren't upset. They were happy with us. Ecstatic, in fact. The numbers went through the roof on yesterday's show. The ratings jumped so much that it broke records. Advertisers are ringing the phone off the hook wanting to book ad time. Tom has pretty much given us carte blanche to do what we want."

"Good. Because I've got something different in mind for today's show...."

HEATHER LEANED CLOSE to the mike, cleared her throat, then began.

"Welcome to *Love on the Rocks*. We have a very special show today. I've asked my producer to hold the calls during this segment because I need to talk about something first. I want to talk about love.'' Moving the slide, she inserted an applause sound track.

''I've been doing this show for nearly three years now and I'm still learning. But there are some things about love that can't be learned. Because love involves a certain amount of magic and there's just no logical way to explain it. In our high-tech world we tend to focus on step-by-step fix-it directions, as if relationships were computer programs—you follow the instructions and it will work the way it's supposed to. But the human heart doesn't function that way. It's full of mysterious factors.'' This time she selected a brief excerpt from the *Twilight Zone*.

''Who's to say why you fall in love with one person and not another? Sure, scientists have tried to attribute it to everything from pheromones to hormones. But I think it's fate. Meant to be. The precognition of a soul mate, a very special link between two people. Now we might not all be lucky enough to find that one person, and maybe we find someone or something else that makes us happy. There might be several people who could make us happy in a romantic relationship. But my heart tells me that there's only one true soul mate.

''That's not to say that it's a perfect fit, that this other person can take you by the hand and lead you to happiness. Relationships will always require hard work and plenty of communication. Which, I guess, means that there will always be plenty for me to talk about on the air.'' Heather activated the applause sound clip again before deciding to abandon special effects in favor of simply speaking from her heart.

"Those of you who listened to the show yesterday might have guessed that I was a little upset. Okay, more than a little. I'd been deeply hurt by someone I cared about very much and so I fought back. But last night I got to thinking about things. There's a quote by Shakespeare that I've always liked. 'Our remedies oft in ourselves do lie.' Now I don't know if I can remedy what went wrong, but I'll never know if I don't try."

She swallowed nervously before launching ahead. "The thing is, I'm in love with an incredible man, a romantic man, a stubborn man. He's my Dark Knight and I want him to know that I love him. And that I'm sorry I messed things up."

She paused to take a deep breath before continuing. "Now, I never told him I loved him. Not until this moment. And it's unlikely he's listening. Then why am I doing this, you ask yourself? Maybe I wanted to practice saying it in front of hundreds of thousands of my listeners first. Maybe that's less terrifying than saying it to him face-to-face. And I didn't tell him I was sorry. I yelled at him instead. You'd think I'd know better, right? Anyway, I know we don't normally play music on my show, but this is a special occasion and there's one song that expresses what I'm trying to say."

She shoved the slide up, and Elton John's "Sorry Seems To Be The Hardest Word" began. The powerful lyrics brought a lump to her throat.

After the song, Heather noticed one phone line flashing. She'd specifically requested that all calls be held during this portion of the show, but they'd put this one through anyway. On the screen Nita had typed: *Mystery guest on line one. You* must *pick up on pain of death.*

"I've been told that there's a call I have to take, so you can see how long my request to hold calls lasted. This is *Love on the Rocks* and you're on the air, mystery guest. What can I do for you?"

"This is Jason's father. And I think there's something I can do for you."

JASON HAD MISSED the sound of Heather's voice so badly that he'd gone out walking on his lunch hour to get away from the aching emptiness. He'd taken out his portable radio-cassette player and listened to the audiotape of John Grisham's latest blockbuster. But the words aggravated him because they weren't being spoken by Heather.

He didn't just miss her voice, he missed her laughter, her sass. He missed the smell of her perfume, the curve of her warm body nestled against his, her lush mouth welcoming him with eager abandonment.

Muttering under his breath, he shoved the Stop button on the tape he wasn't listening to anyway, and somehow managed to turn on the radio in the process. And there was her voice, filling his ears and his mind with her magic. It took a moment or two for the words she was saying to actually sink in.

"I'm in love with an incredible man, a romantic man, a stubborn man. He's my Dark Knight and I want him to know that I love him. And that I'm sorry I messed things up."

Jason stood stock-still, causing a pedestrian traffic

jam on the crowded street. He was so stunned that he couldn't even comprehend what she said next.

It wasn't until the sound of Elton John's song about being sorry came on the air that Jason belatedly realized what he had to do.

JASON'S DAD? Heather almost freaked as he cheerfully continued, "My wife and I have been listening to your show today. First I wanted to tell you that I'm one of those guys who has M.A.S. You know, that male answering syndrome you talked about yesterday? You were really on a toot. But it was like a kick in the pants. Made me realize what I was doing to my marriage. Anyway, I don't want to bore you with the details, but my wife and I are better than ever now."

Heather didn't know what to say. She'd never dreamed that Jason's parents might be listening. "I'm glad to hear that."

"And I wanted to tell you that you've got guts, going on the air and telling my son you love him. We didn't even know he was your Dark Knight until Anastasia told us. Anyway, I'm looking forward to meeting you someday soon. Now don't you give up on him, you hear?"

"I hear. Thanks for calling."

Heather barely had time to recover from that call when her screen lit up again, with more instructions from Nita. *Pick up line two.*

"I guess we have another mystery guest. Hello, caller, you're on *Love on the Rocks*. What can I do for you?" She frowned at the fuzzy response she got.

"I can hardly hear you, caller. Can you speak up a little? And make sure to turn off your radio or you'll hear a delayed echo." Maybe that was why she could hardly hear him.

"I said I've never done this before—called in on a radio program. But your story touched me and I thought that just maybe the guy you were talking about might perhaps have been...a bit of a jerk. Are you there?"

Heather couldn't believe it. It was Jason's voice! She wanted to laugh and cry. Putting her trembling fingers to her mouth, she tried to stifle her breathless gasp, but it went over the airwaves anyway. Finally, she was able to speak. "Yes, I'm still here, Dark Knight. I'm so glad you called. There are things I need to say, *want* to say. And I want to get this right, because it's the most important thing I've ever done. I'm sorry about what happened. You'll never know how sorry. Well, maybe you will know if you stick around for the next fifty years or so."

"Can I get a word in edgewise here?"

"Of course. I'm talking too much, aren't I? I do that when I get nervous. You know that. But I'm talking again. It's your turn. Talk. Talk to me."

"You and your millions of listeners."

"Okay, listeners, turn your radio volume down, this is going to get personal."

Of course, the volumes went up on radios all over Chicago, and another thousand people tuned in when ordered to by friends and relatives who told them, "You won't believe what's going on!"

"There, go ahead, Dark Knight. Talk to me."

"Case law I can take. Prosecuting criminals, presenting my case in front of a jury, these things I can handle. But you—you rattle me."

Her heart sank. "And you don't like being rattled."

"I didn't at first. But then a funny thing happened. You happened. You stole into my heart and you got to me. I can't believe I'm talking to you over the air."

"I can't believe it, either. Where are you calling from?"

A tap on the broadcasting-booth window leading to the hallway had Heather looking over her shoulder in surprise. Jason was standing there, right there, only a few feet away, his dark hair falling over his forehead as if he'd rushed to get to her side as quickly as possible.

"I'm right here. And there's something I have to tell you." As he spoke on the phone, Jason's dark eyes looked directly into hers, melting the glass between them. "I love you, too. More than you'll ever know. But if you stick around for the next fifty years or so, maybe you'll find out."

"I can't wait." Heather's voice was husky with anticipation as she immediately activated the buzzer that unlocked the door from the hallway into the booth.

A second later, Jason was inside the broadcast booth and she was in his arms. Jason kissed her with a passion that rendered her speechless, in what was later referred to as "the kiss heard around the world."

For Heather, it was a kiss that was a merging of souls as well as lips, righting the wrong of their separation. His mouth enclosed hers in a slow, erotic seduction of her senses, adoring her with a tenderness that stole her breath and touched her heart.

Seeing that Heather wasn't going to be doing any talking for a few minutes, Nita, ever the producer, realized that the Elton John compact disc was still ready to go. To the sound of applause from around the station, she played Elton John's classic love song "The One."

"I TOLD YOU they'd come to their senses." Hattie sniffed away the tears of relief, daintily dabbing at the corners of her eyes with a hanky that matched her peach dress. Actual peaches rested atop her big straw hat as she hovered above the console table.

"Sure, go ahead and rub it in, Miss Smarty-pants." Despite her tart words, Betty's eyes weren't exactly dry, either. On her T-shirt were the words If Fairy Godmomma Ain't Happy, Ain't Nobody Happy.

"You have to admit that they did work things out themselves."

"They certainly did. It's enough to renew my faith in human nature," Betty noted with uncharacteristic sentimentality.

Leaving it to Muriel to be the practical fairy godmother. "One down, two to go. Now let's go work on Ryan...."

* * * * *

Don't miss TOO STUBBORN TO MARRY
Love & Laughter #45 in June 1998.

LOVE & LAUGHTER™

Marriage Makers

by
Cathie Linz

Once upon a time, three bumbling fairy god-mothers set out to find the Knight triplets their soul mates. But... Jason was too sexy, Ryan was too stubborn and Anastasia was just too smart to settle down.

But with the perfect match and a little fairy dust...
Happily Ever After is just a wish away!

March 1998—
TOO SEXY FOR MARRIAGE (#39)

June 1998—
TOO STUBBORN TO MARRY (#45)

September 1998—
TOO SMART FOR MARRIAGE (#51)

Available wherever Harlequin books are sold.

Look us up on-line at: http://www.romance.net   HLLMM

shocking
pink

THEY WERE ONLY WATCHING…

The mysterious lovers the three girls spied on were engaged in
a deadly sexual game no one else was supposed to know about.
Especially not Andie and her friends whose curiosity had deepened into a dangerous obsession.…

Now fifteen years later, Andie is being watched by someone who
won't let her forget the unsolved murder of "Mrs. X" or the
sudden disappearance of "Mr. X." And Andie doesn't know who
her friends are.…

WHAT THEY SAW WAS MURDER.

ERICA
SPINDLER

Available in February 1998 at your favorite retail outlet.

**The Brightest Stars
in Women's Fiction.™**

Look us up on-line at: http://www.romance.net   MES415

**Look for these titles—
available at your favorite retail outlet!**

January 1998
Renegade Son by Lisa Jackson
Danielle Summers had problems: a rebellious child
and unscrupulous enemies. In addition, her Montana
ranch was slowly being sabotaged. And then there was
Chase McEnroe—who admired her land and desired her
body. But Danielle feared he would invade more than just
her property—he'd trespass on her heart.

February 1998
The Heart's Yearning by Ginna Gray
Fourteen years ago Laura gave her baby up for adoption,
and not one day had passed that she didn't think about
him and agonize over her choice—so she finally followed
her heart to Texas to see her child. But the plan to watch
her son from afar doesn't quite happen that way, once the
boy's sexy—*single*—father takes a decided interest in *her*.

March 1998
First Things Last by Dixie Browning
One look into Chandler Harrington's dark eyes and
Belinda Massey could refuse the Virginia millionaire nothing.
So how could the no-nonsense nanny believe the rumors that
he had kidnapped his nephew—an adorable, healthy little boy
who crawled as easily into her heart as he did into her lap?

**BORN IN THE USA: Love, marriage—
and the pursuit of family!**

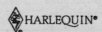 

Look us up on-line at: http://www.romance.net

BESTSELLING AUTHORS
IN THE SPOTLIGHT

.WE'RE SHINING THE SPOTLIGHT
ON SIX OF OUR STARS!

**Harlequin and Silhouette have selected stories
from several of their bestselling authors to give
you six sensational reads. These star-powered
romances are bound to please!**

THERE'S A PRICE TO PAY FOR STARDOM…
AND IT'S LOW

As a special offer, these six outstanding
books are available from Harlequin and
Silhouette for only $1.99 in the U.S. and
$2.50 in Canada. Watch for these titles:

At the Midnight Hour—**Alicia Scott**

Joshua and the Cowgirl—**Sherryl Woods**

Another Whirlwind Courtship—**Barbara Boswell**

Madeleine's Cowboy—**Kristine Rolofson**

Her Sister's Baby—**Janice Kay Johnson**

One and One Makes Three—**Muriel Jensen**

Available in March 1998
at your favorite retail outlet.

PBAIS

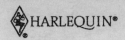

Not The Same Old Story!

Exciting, glamorous romance stories that take readers around the world.

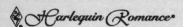

Sparkling, fresh and tender love stories that bring you pure romance.

Bold and adventurous— Temptation is strong women, bad boys, great sex!

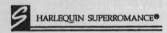

Provocative and realistic stories that celebrate life and love.

Contemporary fairy tales—where anything is possible and where dreams come true.

Heart-stopping, suspenseful adventures that combine the best of romance and mystery.

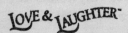

Humorous and romantic stories that capture the lighter side of love.

Look us up on-line at: http://www.romance.net   HGENERIC

DEBBIE MACOMBER

invites you to the

HEART OF TEXAS

Join Debbie Macomber as she brings you the lives
and loves of the folks in the ranching community
of Promise, Texas.

If you loved Midnight Sons—don't miss
Heart of Texas! A brand-new six-book series
from Debbie Macomber.

Available in February 1998
at your favorite retail store.

Heart of Texas by Debbie Macomber

Lonesome Cowboy	February '98
Texas Two-Step	March '98
Caroline's Child	April '98
Dr. Texas	May '98
Nell's Cowboy	June '98
Lone Star Baby	July '98

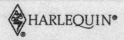
HARLEQUIN®

HPHRT1

Don't miss these Harlequin favorites by some of our top-selling authors!

HT#25733	THE GETAWAY BRIDE	$3.50 U.S. ☐	
	by Gina Wilkins	$3.99 CAN. ☐	
HP#11849	A KISS TO REMEMBER	$3.50 U.S. ☐	
	by Miranda Lee	$3.99 CAN. ☐	
HR#03431	BRINGING UP BABIES	$3.25 U.S. ☐	
	by Emma Goldrick	$3.75 CAN. ☐	
HS#70723	SIDE EFFECTS	$3.99 U.S. ☐	
	by Bobby Hutchinson	$4.50 CAN. ☐	
HI#22377	CISCO'S WOMAN	$3.75 U.S. ☐	
	by Aimée Thurlo	$4.25 CAN. ☐	
HAR#16666	ELISE & THE HOTSHOT LAWYER	$3.75 U.S. ☐	
	by Emily Dalton	$4.25 CAN. ☐	
HH#28949	RAVEN'S VOW	$4.99 U.S. ☐	
	by Gayle Wilson	$5.99 CAN. ☐	

(limited quantities available on certain titles)

AMOUNT	$ _____
POSTAGE & HANDLING	$ _____
($1.00 for one book, 50¢ for each additional)	
APPLICABLE TAXES*	$ _____
TOTAL PAYABLE	$ _____

(check or money order—please do not send cash)

To order, complete this form and send it, along with a check or money order for the total above, payable to Harlequin Books, to: **In the U.S.:** 3010 Walden Avenue, P.O. Box 9047, Buffalo, NY 14269-9047; **In Canada:** P.O. Box 613, Fort Erie, Ontario, L2A 5X3.

Name: _____

Address: _____ City: _____

State/Prov.: _____ Zip/Postal Code: _____

Account Number (if applicable): _____

*New York residents remit applicable sales taxes.
 Canadian residents remit applicable GST and provincial taxes.

Look us up on-line at: http://www.romance.net

075-CSAS

HBLJM98